Primrose's
life is marked by
the absence of her mother.

My own has been blessed by the presence of a
particularly good one. Mammy Sullivan, this one's
for you ... and also my Dad, Tim, who is brave and clever
and funny and has been sporting a moustache since
before they were cool.

Thanks for having me, guys. It's
lovely to be here.

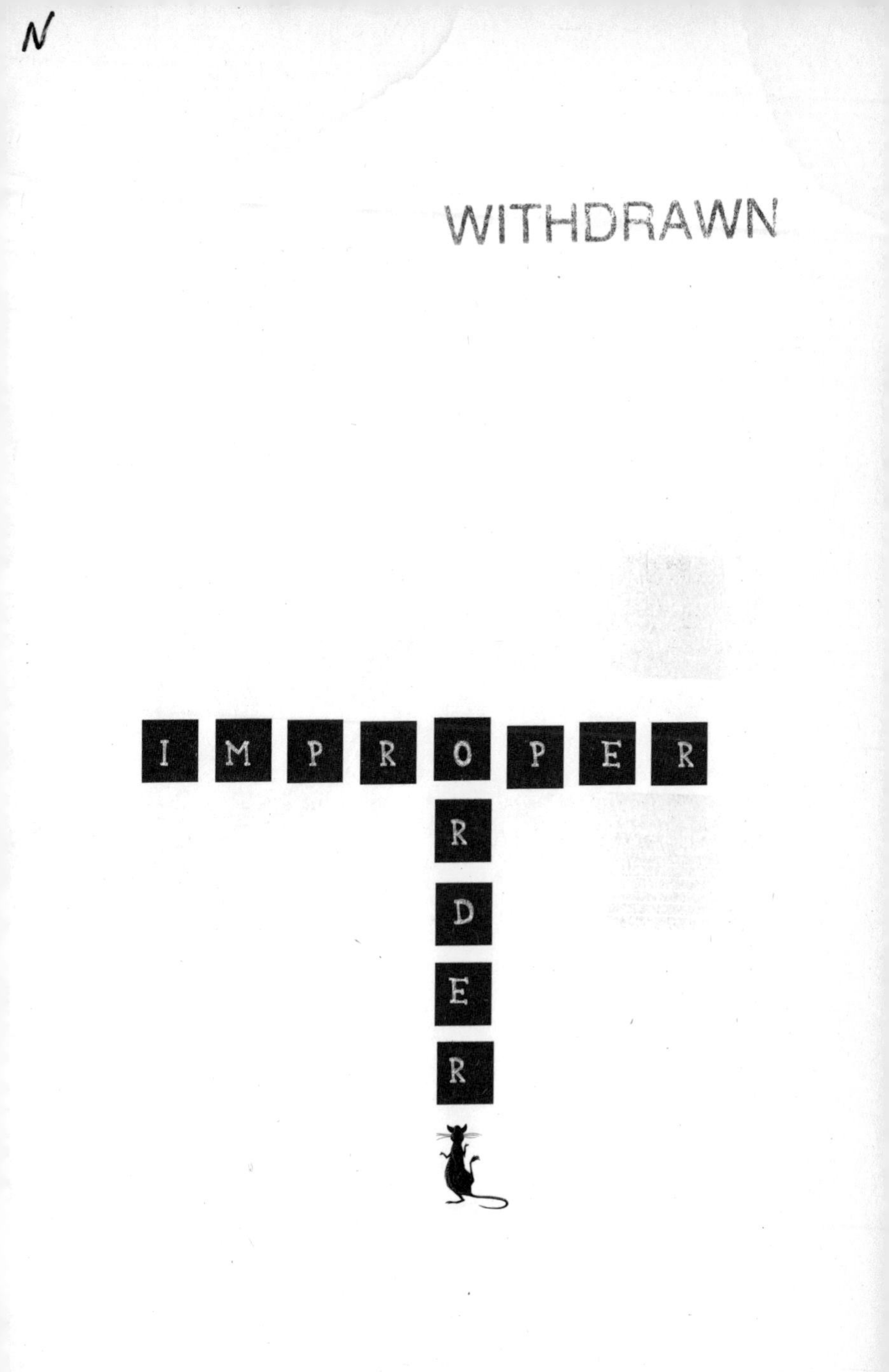
IMPROPER
ORDER

Also by this author

**PRIM IMPROPER**

IMPROPER
ORDER
by
Deirdre
Sullivan

Little Island

IMPROPER ORDER
Published 2013
by Little Island
7 Kenilworth Park
Dublin 6W
Ireland

www.littleisland.ie



ISBN 978-1-908195-23-4



British Library Cataloguing Data. A CIP catalogue record for this book is available from the British Library.

Design by Fidelma Slattery @ Someday.ie

Typeset in Baskerville. Cover typefaces: 'Denne Milk Tea' by Denise Bentulan and 'Agent C' by Carl Leisegang, also used throughout the interior along with 'Denne Freakshow' by Denise Bentulan.

Printed in Poland by Drukarnia Skleniarz

Little Island receives financial assistance from
The Arts Council (An Chomhairle Ealaíon), Dublin, Ireland.

10 9 8 7 6 5 4 3 2

# A NOTE FROM THE PUBLISHER

Just in case you haven't read *Prim Improper* (sad thought, but these things happen ...) here's a bit of background info to get you up and running.

Primrose Leary is fourteen years old and goes to secondary school. Her lovely mum, Bláthnaid, was knocked off her bicycle and killed by a hit-and-run driver a year or two ago. Now Prim lives with her dad, Fintan, in his swanky house.

Prim and Fintan do not always see eye to eye, but they are getting along better these days than they did when Prim first moved in with him. (Read *Prim Improper* if you want to know how bad it was at first. Or, hey, just read *Prim Improper* anyway.)

OK, that's enough, because, look, we can't be explaining everything. We trust you to be able to work out a few things for yourself. But fret not: the other people (and rat) in the story are explained as you go along.

Oh, yes, and the 'chapter titles' are crossword clues. You don't have to solve them unless you want to. Anyway, the truly perspicacious among you will also be able to find where the solutions are hidden.

**PERSPICACIOUS:** Has the same meaning as the word smart, but it's longer and more impressive.

## PLUMP PATERNAL WOMAN (6)

When I grow up I want to be a cruciverbalist. Fintan thinks that this is no sort of a job at all, but seeing as his job consists of making more and more money for people who are already far too rich for their own good, his opinion is a bit redundant.

His title now is 'Director of Operations', which would be impressive except they aren't real operations, like transplants or nose-jobs, and he isn't the real director of anything useful, like a play or a film or even a silly little Christmas pageant like we had in primary school. I understand, of course, that he is not *that kind* of director, but when I pretend not to understand that, he gets all frustrated and sighs heavily and eventually his moustache begins to flutter like a big black scrubbing brush that is ruffled by a gentle summer breeze.

> **CRUCIVERBALIST:** Someone who designs crosswords for a living. What I am thinking of being when I grow up. Although it may not last. A fortnight ago, I was going to be an organic farmer because of all the food and adorable wellingtons I would have.

The reason I want to be a cruciverbalist is not because it sounds like some sort of dark wizard (although that is one of many amazing perks). No, I want to do it because I have started doing the crosswords in *The Irish Times* and they are hard. Like, crazy hard. Except for the Simplex, because it has simple in the title and so I refuse to let it defeat me. So one day, when I had only gotten two of the cryptic clues, it occurred to me how amazing it would be to be the maker-upper of the puzzles, how pleased you would feel when people worked them out and how smug you would feel when they failed to do so.

So I started making up my own crossword clues, and it is kind of the most fun I have had by myself in ages. And it turns out it is an actual job. There's no college course for it, but I will learn my skills from the University of Life. (I also plan to go to real university, but all my talk about the University of Life is really getting on Fintan's wick, so that is why I keep going on about it when he's in the room.)

In real life, I think I might want to do journalism in college. Because then I could get a job at a newspaper and make sure their chief cruciverbalist has an accident so I can rise up to assume his or her place. The good thing about this plan is that you can repeat it as required, like with a shampoo, so if there are any other budding cruciverbalists at my place of work, I could take them down as well. I can do this by sneaky stairs-pushing or germ warfare, in which I catch a nasty cold and make out with all my enemies in order to pass it on to them.

But before I become evil, I have to have the skills to back it up. I have to study and hone and do lots of crosswords so I can understand their language and use it to my own nefarious ends. My ends are not always nefarious, only sometimes they can be. But not, like, crazy nefarious. More mildly nefarious. Divilish, as opposed to devilish. Because being a divil isn't the worst thing in the world you can be, but being *the* Devil is not a good thing at all.

**NEFARIOUS:** Evil. People who are nefarious include Stalin, Hitler, Pol-Pot (in spite of his funny name) and The Devil Himself. Also Karen. Especially Karen, as a matter of fact.

**GETTING ON SOMEONE'S WICK:** This is like getting on someone's goat, if they have a wick instead of a goat. I am always getting onto people's goats and wicks. It is kind of a problem.

**DIVIL:** Lovable rogue. Not to be confused with the actual Devil.

**KAREN:** Karen is a horrible person. She used to be friends with my friend Ciara, before Ciara was my friend Ciara, but then she started doing this whole excludey kind of business that a certain type of mean and nefarious individual is so good at. Also, there was this whole thing last year where I punched her in the face for calling my friend Ella a 'starey little retard'. Ella has Asperger's syndrome, which makes her a little bit different from most people I know, but in a way I appreciate and love. Karen is a lot different from most people I know as well because she was born without a soul. She is pretty much a sociopath, I reckon. The only reason I regret punching her in the face is because it dragged me down to her level.

**SOCIOPATH:** Someone who is born without a sense of empathy. They cannot relate to other human beings, and if they pretend to do so it is only because they are up to something. Serial killers and Karen are often sociopaths. Some cut-throat businessmen are as well, but my dad Fintan isn't one, even if I sometimes think he is because he has no idea what I'm feeling half the time.

Anyway, if I wanted to be the Devil I would have to push Karen down the stairs and take her job. That girl is nefarious personified. She broke Simone's iPod Touch yesterday by throwing it out a top-floor window, just to see what would happen.

Simone is one of Karen's good friends. Imagine how she would treat an enemy. I don't have to imagine, because she hates my guts. Luckily, I do not have an iPod Touch. I'd love an iPod Touch. Fintan is mean and does not shower me with enough gifts.

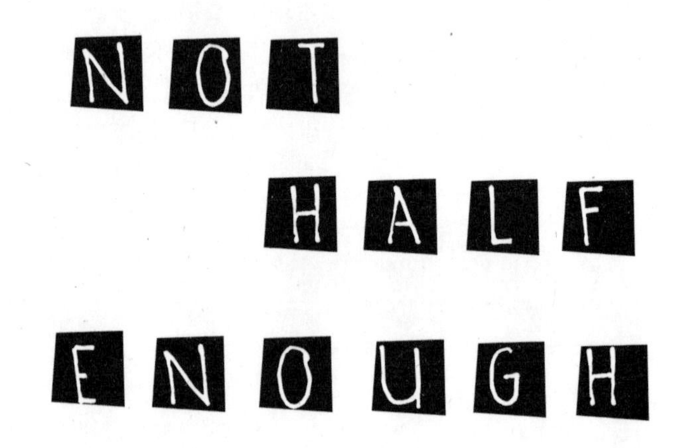

# FATHER

Things never really go away, do they? They lurk and lie in wait like wolves. Horrible, un-fluffy, lurk-in-the-darkness wolves. The kind that would never swallow a girl whole but chew her up to mincey dog-breath spit, so if a woodcutter happened to slice open its wolfish tummy the last thing he would find is a happy ending.

Happy endings are pretty rare. The most people get if they're lucky is a happy beginning. I didn't even get that. Mum and Dad were hardly on speaking terms when I was born. I was the little wailing white flag of truce. Or so they told me (though not in those exact words, obviously).

Really, I think it is just easier to try to get along than to stay mad at someone for an indeterminate length of time. I mean, being angry for more than a brief period of time takes effort. You have to work at it. And what if the person you are angry with says something hilarious or offers you a delicious treat of some kind? Let's say, for argument's sake, a caramel slice and a cup of tea. It is hard to stay angry at somebody when you are eating something delicious that they have bought in the cool deli place adjacent to their work which wraps their treats in fancy pink and white paper.

Fintan is lucky that that deli exists, is all I am saying. Because otherwise having a teenage daughter would be a whole lot harder for him.

**HEDDA:** My father's girlfriend. She is far too glamorous for the likes of him. She used to have braids, but she recently got them taken out. Her hair is in this beautiful curly afro-bob now and I really want to touch it, but I can't ask her for permission to do so, because that would be weird, right? That would be incredibly no-way-am-I-ever-going-to-marry-into-that-creepy-creepy-family weird.

The reason I was angry with him was to do with him forgetting to pick me up from swimming class. I'd left two notes on the fridge and texted him in the morning to remind him.

But instead he went on a date with Hedda and turned his phone off. Hedda was angry with him too. You see, he is always taking phone calls from important people while they are going places. Once he even left in the middle of a play to talk to a man in China about something. Hedda believes that if you are going to spend time with someone, you should actually spend time with them, instead of ignoring them and doing important businessman-type stuff like talking about mergers and stock portfolios and indices.

See, the weird thing is that money isn't even real. It is, like, this fictional concept we all agree on to make the transfer of goods and services flow more smoothly. Mum's friend Sorrel once went to live in a commune where they used swapping and kindness instead of money. It didn't really work, though, because once the swapping got heated, the kindness kind of went down the pan. She was the one who explained to me about money being made up and stuff. I mean, they are just bits of metal and paper. The only value they have is the one that we assign to them.

Sorrel was the person who dropped me home after I had been waiting on my own an hour outside a now-closing swimming pool. She was the only one who was picking up her phone, which is weird because she normally doesn't even have it switched on. She was waiting for a call from this nice organic farmer she met at a drumming circle. When she told me this, I did an eye-roll and her eyes filled with tears and she told me that I had just done my mother's 'Oh, for the love of God' face.

She waited with me in the kitchen till about eleven o' clock. Dad still wasn't home, but I wanted to go to bed because I had school in the morning and stuff. Luckily, I had got my homework done at Mary's before swimming because I would have been too angry to do it afterwards.

**SORREL:** My mum's friend and a notorious proponent of all that is alternative and hippified. She does things like offer you Manuka honey and make her own hummus. I like her, but I do not believe in homeopathy.

**HOMEOPATHY:** This thing that masquerades as alternative medicine but does not actually do anything. You put a drop of whatever ails you in water and then dilute it a lot and then use it to cure you of maladies. It doesn't work.

Sometimes I forget how useless Fintan is at this whole being-a-father business. Luckily, he is always ready to

**MARY:** Ella's (and my beloved Felix's) mum. I stay at her house after school most weekdays because Dad is too busy having a job to be a pick-your-daughter-up-from-school sort of dad. I like staying at Mary's because of Felix and Ella and also because Mary is nice. I resent the hell out of being babysat, though. I am a grown-ass adolescent and should be left alone to become isolated and neglected and eventually experiment with drugs and performance poetry. Dad is fencing me in with all this babysitting, coming-home-to-friendship-and-a-warm-plate-of-food malarkey

remind me with some new and stupid mishap. At least he didn't bring up the time I stole the engagement ring he got for Hedda. See, a year and a half ago, Dad almost proposed to Hedda on a trip to New York. Only he couldn't – because I had taken the engagement ring from its little box in a perfectly understandable fit of wanting to be told if my dad was going to make any life-changing decisions.

I still don't think I was wholly in the wrong. If it were the right thing for Dad, he would have proposed anyway. It's not like the ring is hyper-important. When Mum's friend Méadhbh was proposed to by her husband Frank, he did not have a ring at all, just a receipt he rolled into a ring shape. They picked the ring together later, because as lovely and spontaneous as a rolled up receipt from IKEA is, it would be a touch impractical for everyday wear.

Anyway, Dad should probably have proposed when he got the ring back, or on any number of occasions over the past year or so. I apologised and stuff – I mean, he was quite irate when he got back from his holiday – but

I think that time has told that I was in the right. Anyway, ever since I did that small bit of misappropriation, he has brought it up every time he does something wrong. Which is all the bloody time. Except this time. Which means one of the following:

1. He has gotten over himself about it and acknowledges that it was a clever and awesome move on my part.

2. He recognises that what he did this time was worse than what I did that time.

3. Hedda gave out to him about it.

When Hedda gives out, Fintan listens. This is one of her superpowers: the ability to make my thick-as-muck-in-terms-of-human-emotion father understand what he did wrong and accept responsibility for it. It is why I both like and fear her more than any of my dad's previous girlfriends – like, because when her powers are used for good (most of the time) they can be kind of amazing; fear, because what if she uses them against me one fine day? I mean, there is a DISTINCT possibility that she will one day become my stepmother and have to give out to me about things on a semi-regular basis. Which I do not think I would like even a little bit. Because she has this way of being right and I have this way of liking to be right and I do not think that the two would complement each other very well at all at all.

Anyway, I did not speak to Fintan for three days after the whole swimming incident. Because going to swimming lessons is troubling enough when you are a teenage girl with body hair and a healthy distrust of skin-tight fabrics. There is no reason for Fintan to make it more troubling than it already is. Although the insecure bits normally happen outside of the water. Once I'm in there, I get all focused and splashy and usually enjoy myself.

Which is a good thing, because I don't really like other sports. When hand–eye coordination was given out, I must have been in the corner reading a book or something. I am not good at hitting balls with sticks or kicking them into nets or throwing them into baskets. But in swimming, it's not about racing other people or whatever, it's about beating your own best time, and even though there are plenty of people in my group who are better than me (mainly Laura, the human dolphin), for some reason I can kind of block them out, the way I do the world when I'm reading a good book, and just do my best. This is rare for me. Which is just one of the many, many reasons that I should not be driven to associate the swimming pool with abandonment and so on and so forth.

Fintan did apologise right away. But I kind of want to reinforce that it is never OK to forget you have a daughter, especially when you are the only parent that she has left. Ooh, I should totally say that to him; it will make him feel terrible. Which will teach him not to do it in future. This is a really nice caramel slice. He is lucky I do not have an eating disorder. Because how would he win me around then?

Probably money.

**MERGER:** When two companies join forces to become one company. Except sometimes the smaller company doesn't want to merge, but the big company makes it merge anyway in the name of business. Mergers make people incredibly stressed out about things going 'down the pan', which is a phrase Fintan says a lot when he is worried.

**GOING DOWN THE PAN:** Becoming messed up, going to the dogs. Neither of these phrases makes a lot of sense, as things can go in the pan, and sometimes even out of the frying pan into the fire, but how can they go down it? I have never seen a pan that has a plughole like a sink. They have flat, smooth bottoms, and while one can sometimes burn things that are in the pan, they generally don't fall down anywhere and disappear.

**GIVE OUT TO:** Hiberno-English for scold, berate, upbraid, chide and many other unpleasantries.

**HIBERNO-ENGLISH:** English as it is spoken in Ireland (which is to say, better).

## ROOT VEGETABLE FOR THE BOOKS (6)

I think I have grown up a lot this year. Sometimes I feel like a completely different person – one with boobs (34 B!!) and a mature and rational outlook on life and matters sociological.

Of course, it is hard to be mature when all around you are kind of losing the plot. Fintan wants to make Hedda his bride, but he is not going about it the right way at all – he cancels plans with her all the time in order to stay in his counting house, counting all his money like a king in a nursery rhyme.

I am now the go-to girl for relationship advice. The moustache-sporting man of men actually trusts me, for some reason. My advice is to stop cancelling plans because girls do not like that. I don't like it when Joel or Ciara cancel plans on me and they are just friends. Imagine how bad it would feel if I were to have a lover do it to me. Fintan stopped me there and told me he did not want to imagine me having a lover doing anything to me and also that I was not allowed to have lovers until I was older.

**JOEL:** My best friend since playschool. Joel is one of the parts of my life that makes me feel luckiest. Last year he was in a different school, but now he goes to my school which is working out marvellously for fun-having, but not so well for attention-paying. Joel is very good at sports but does not like them because he doesn't see the point. He quite likes to watch people playing sports, though. Particularly rugby.

Anyway, I told him that if he did not pop the question within the week, then I would do it for him, the way Joel put a profile for his little brother Marcus on an online dating website, just for fun, until his parents found out about it and got really angry.

Marcus actually got a lot of attention, which is weird, as his profile picture was him (a three-year-old boy) dressed as Wall-E (a robot; Marcus likes robots). The teachers in primary school were all too right about the dangers of the Internet. There are a lot of scary adults out there. Luckily, Marcus had Joel to vet his potential suitors for him and weed out any creeps. At least he did till Joel's dad, Liam, sat down with us and supervised the deletion of the profile. We did say on the site that he was thirty-eight, which was true, only in months not years. Not that I had much of a hand in it, apart from convincing Joel to give fake contact information.

Liam was FURIOUS with the two of us and made us apologise to Marcus, even though he was too young to understand what was going on. Joel was made to mow the lawn from then till Easter, join a hurling team and start Mixed Martial Arts lessons as a punishment. He is not mad about hurling, but the MMA has grown on him. Liam coaches the hurling team, and I think he needed more members. He is always trying to get Joel to do sports. I think this probably contributes to Joel's distaste for doing sports.

Anne's punishment was to get him to design and make a new robot costume for Marcus and to install a program that filters out any website with unsuitable material on it unless you put in a security code. Joel really needs to find out what that security code is. We can't even look at recipes for chicken ('HOT CHICK') or watch that six-membered group of ukulele players we like so much ('SEXTET'). It really is most inconvenient.

Also, they told Fintan and he was going to install the same thing, only he didn't have the time and then forgot about it. Joel was really annoyed at getting caught out, but he didn't complain much about the many, many, many punishments that were heaped upon him once the jig was up. He is good at taking it on the chin. Joel's weird like that. If I have something to complain about I kind of can't help going on and on about it – like when Fintan forgot to pick me up that time, I texted Joel and Ciara and even Ella to let them know what a tool he was being. Important information, in my opinion.

I don't talk much about Mum dying, though. Not that I hide it from people or anything – that would have been quite difficult, what with the funeral and everything – but I didn't, like, go on and on about how unfair it was and how much I missed her. How much I still miss her.

Weird that it has been over a year now since she died. I have had two birthdays. I am fourteen and a half. My hair has been two different colours and, for a brief period, in lots and lots of those little fancy plaits that Hedda does so well. I wear a bra now and I get my period, but not every twenty-eight days like the internet says you are supposed to. It comes about once every six weeks. I asked the GP, and she said it would probably settle into a more regular pattern when I was a bit older. Mum would have done the asking for me, if she was around. I wouldn't have had to pretend to have a chest infection to justify a trip to the surgery. So I suppose that was another problem I didn't talk about. Except to the doctor. And to Ciara. And to Joel, until he stuck his fingers in his ears and began to sing the national anthem.

I assume Fintan knows that I am menstruating like a grown-up lady, though. He is very good about me missing swimming the odd week. I don't know why Joel is so disgusted by the idea of me having a period. I mean, every woman does, or almost every woman anyway. I know that the thought of it is a bit gross. So is the reality of it, to be honest. It takes a bit of getting used to. And it's hard to know what's normal and what isn't. I mean, in sixth class everyone was all 'Have you got yours yet?', like it was this REALLY BIG DEAL. And now I think we pretty much all have them but we don't talk about it any more. Which sucks, because I still have some questions.

So now I am a proper time-of-the-month-having woman, which means I am biologically equipped to start having loads and loads of lovely grandchildren for my beloved papa to take care of till I finish college.

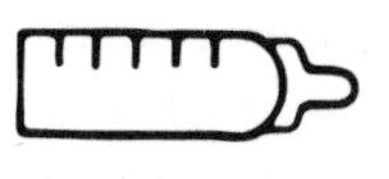

Note to self: Do not start having loads and loads of lovely grandchildren for Fintan to take care of until I finish college. I think the past year and a half has established that Fintan is not the best at child-rearing. I mean, he flounders and flaps around the place trying to look after a fourteen-year-old girl. My future babies would probably not last long if left to his tender mercies. One by one they would be abandoned at swimming pools and supermarkets, playgrounds and crèches. It would suck for them because they would not be equipped with grown-up survival tools like mobile phones and bus money.

I could almost well up thinking about all my poor abandoned little illegitimate babies. I am also illegitimate. It is not a very nice word and was mostly used when priests used to put single mothers in homes and made them do laundry and gave their babies to rich married people. Mum took me to see a film about that kind of thing once, and after crying most of the way through it, we decided not to do laundry for a fortnight to honour the poor abandoned mums and their stolen babies. The great laundry boycott lasted a week and a half, until I ran out of socks.

Fintan never does anything fun like that, mostly because he has the cleaning lady to do his laundry. Sometimes I put on a load or two, but if he sees me doing it, he gives out to me because I don't put enough dirty clothes into the machine and that is a big waste of energy.

He once asked me why I couldn't put the dark things in as well, to save water. Then I had to explain to him about dyes running and things turning different colours and so on. The next day, he produced a small wrapped package from his bag. 'This is for you,' he said. When I opened it, it was a box of things called

Colour Catchers. I thanked him, but I haven't tried them out yet. I am not sure that I trust them. Maybe when I wash my red dress with the cream collar and cuffs I will use one. I don't know why he wrapped it, though. It was not the kind of present one usually wraps, and when I opened it I was kind of disappointed.

Fintan has a lot to learn about present giving. Also about proposing to his girlfriend. At one stage, he was thinking about putting the ring in Hedda's dessert in a fancy restaurant. I told him that this was a sucky idea for two reasons.

## ONE

She almost always orders sticky toffee pudding, so the ring would get all dirty, and you don't want sticky brown smears to feature in your proposal story.

Proposing in a public place would put Hedda in a really awkward position if she wanted to turn Fintan down. (Fintan didn't like this reason very much because I don't think it had occurred to him that she might not be thoroughly delighted by the prospect of spending the rest of her life tied to him and him alone. He is very confident.) Because people would be watching and so on and so forth as she broke his businessman's heart into a million little pieces with her cruel, cruel words. The decision to marry is deeply personal and should not be affected by smirking waiters and patrons going 'Aww'.

I think Fintan should go the traditional route of taking her to a secluded spot of great natural beauty where they can gaze at the horizon happily or, if it goes badly, have a blazing row without anyone around to hear them.

Ciara and I were talking about proposals the other day. She has already designed her wedding dress: it has three-quarter-length sleeves, a low standy-up collar, a sweetheart neckline and a sweeping skirt. She is not a fan of trains because you have to get flower girls to hold them up and kids' hands are always filthy.

She asked me about the cut of the ring. I did not know that rings had different cuts. Shapes, yes, but cuts? Fintan has chosen an elegant solitaire, apparently. Ciara can see why he would go for that, but she prefers a princess cut herself, more for the name than the look. 'Every bride should be a princess' is her motto.

I do not think that every bride should be a princess. Because I think princesses are a bit passé. Also, I am my father's little princess and, even though I do not let him call me that any more without rolling my eyes to heaven, I do not want him to have another princess. He has not called me his little princess in ages, actually. Maybe Hedda is his princess now. She does look a bit regal, so I suppose it makes sense.

Ciara cannot believe it has taken Fintan so long to get around to proposing. Her dad proposed to her mum after six months of going out. And Fintan and Hedda have been going out for almost two years now.

'By that logic, Ciara,' I said, 'Syzmon should have proposed to you already.' At which she laughed and then looked a bit worried and said, 'Why hasn't he?'

I told her that

1. They were both far too young.
2. He probably couldn't afford a princess-cut diamond ring of sufficient quality.

She wasn't really convinced by 1. because 'we could have a really long engagement, until it was legal and stuff'. But number 2. made 'a LOT of sense'. Sometimes I despair of Ciara. She will probably end up married at eighteen to a professional footballer to facilitate her love of luxury.

**SOCIOLOGICAL:** To do with society. Basically the way we live and interact with each other. If you study this, then you are a sociologist and might be called to give your opinion as part of a tacky documentary about social problems like teenagers running amok and all the drugs and pregnancies they are taking and having. If you are a good sociologist, you will probably steer clear of that sort of thing, though. I mean, who has the time?

**BOYCOTT:** Having nothing to do with whatever you are boycotting. If you boycott a shop, you don't shop there any more on principle. If you boycott a particular brand of cheese, you do not put it in any sandwiches whatsoever. People often do this sort of thing on principle, like if the cheese was made out of poor people's kidneys as well as milk, or something. That is a disgusting thought. I would definitely boycott kidney cheese.

**TRAIN:** Not the choo-choo kind. Like a long, sweeping piece of dress that trails elegantly after you. Usually found on wedding dresses and ballgowns. Not usually found on school uniforms, unless you attend a school for Disney princesses.

**SOLITAIRE:** A one-player card game. Dad often plays a computer version of it when he is in the middle of working on very important documents. When you win, the cards swoop and swoosh around in a dance of joyous victory and it is really gratifying. He says it makes him feel like he has accomplished something and can go on to accomplish more, which is apparently a good frame of mind to be in, in his line of work. But it is also a cut of a diamond on jewellery. It's probably the one that pops into your head as soon as you think of engagement rings because practically all of them are solitaire.

## TURNIP

I am kind of obsessed with Laura, this girl from my swimming class. Not in a bad way – I just kind of want her life. She is an amazing swimmer and has these really effortless good looks: honey-blond hair and clear, clear skin. I have never, ever seen her with a spot. Not once. And her swimsuit has a really low back.

She is very friendly but, like all human dolphins, she does tend to squeak a lot, particularly if anything exciting is told to her. She gets straight As, which I do too, but she is super popular as well and her friends throw house parties and take each other on holidays when they go. Fintan would never think of inviting Joel or Ciara to go on holidays with him. Or me, for that matter. He goes on holidays with Hedda; I get minded. Such is the way of the world.

Laura's parents have an apartment in France. Because her mum is French. Did I mention she has both a mum and a dad and that, by all accounts, they co-exist happily?

Also, her boyfriend Mac is kind of amazing. He looks like a troubled vampire, all pale and lean and angular, and he drives a funky little moped on which he picks her up from swimming every week. Mac is always giving her presents, but not lavish ones, really thoughtful ones. Like goggles that don't let the water in or a jar of red and purple Skittles. (Laura only likes the red and purple Skittles.) When Mac and Laura are together, they look like an ad for a perfume called 'Perfection'. Or 'Happiness'.

But the thing I am most jealous of about Laura is that it is impossible not to like her. She's so friendly and funny and self-deprecating and she genuinely seems interested in people. If I had that kind of life, I think I would assume that everybody else was less fascinating than me and treat him or her accordingly. But she's really sweet and even gave me some of her Skittles, that time Mac gave her Skittles.

I wonder what Mac is short for. Macaulay? Macmillan? MacHandsome? It truly is one of life's great mysteries. One I would like to solve by kissing him all over his lovely mouth. That is, if he wasn't Laura's boyfriend. That is, if a boy that hot would even look at me. Not that it's all about looks. Except it totally is. I haven't even spoken to him once. Unless waving goodbye to Laura as the two of them mopeded off into the sunset together counts. This actually happened once. We got out of swimming just as the sun was setting. It was enough to make me sick. When I told Ciara about it, she kind of shut me down because it is not OK to fancy men who belong to other women. I think she was pre-emptively stopping me from fancying Syzmon. Which I totally never would because looking at Syzmon doesn't make me all fizzy inside, like some sort of sexy lemonade.

Joel is a better person to share boy-fancying with. If he met Mac, he would probably fancy him too. Because he is a human being with eyes. Such is the potency of Mac.

I hate having such an envious nature. I'm jealous of so many people and the things they have. Things like beauty and friends and the easy grace of the world's most adorable sea mammal when they swim. I'm jealous of Ciara for having sleek hair and the kind of perfectly pointed chin that girls in romance novels who end up with attractive knights have.

Having trolled through all of Mum's Viking books, I am now delving into the world of the knight. This is weirdly helping me with my history, because if you leave out the sexy bits, sometimes you find a chilling indictment of the feudal system that gets my essays called 'insightful' by Miss Griffin. Also, they talk a lot about notable battles, even if the only reason for them was to have the hero wounded on his smooth, tanned chest, so the heroine can look at it and bandage his wounds lustfully and sometimes stroke his knightly chest hair.

When I grow up I think I would like to write my PhD thesis on the difference between sexy knights and sexy Vikings. Also their respective cultural impacts. I think it is what Mum would have wanted.

OK, it totally isn't, but doesn't it sound fun?

**PHD THESIS:** When you do a PhD, you have to write a big thing called a thesis. This is about a million words long and can be about anything you want, as long as it is linked to your PhD. When it is finished, you get it bound and then no one but your lecturer ever reads it, according to Mum's friend Méadhbh. And she should know, because she is a doctor of Women's Studies. Which is quite cool, but not very much help when someone is having a heart attack in a restaurant.

**SELF-DEPRECATING:** Being able to recognise your faults and share them with others, often in a humorous manner. This is not to be confused with self-loathing, because self-loathing is a bad thing, but self-deprecating is a good thing. Dolphin Laura is sometimes self-deprecating, and this is lovely, because she is almost perfect, so when she points out her nerdy love of colour-coding study notes or her lack of a skincare regimen, this makes her more relatable. Because I lack a skincare regimen too! Oh, Dolphin Laura, we could be twins! Except I would be the less attractive and talented darkly jealous twin with a whopping crush on my sister's boyfriend.

**CULTURAL IMPACT:** The impact a thing has on culture. Like Michael Jackson had a big cultural impact, because almost everyone knows who he was and he influenced loads of other musicians and dancers and music video directors and people with more money than sense. Laura the Human Dolphin LOVES Michael Jackson. She claims singing 'Beat It' in her head makes her swim faster. I tried it once, but it just made me get water up my nose.

**MUM'S VIKING BOOKS:** One of the things that Mum left behind when she died was a big box of trashy romance novels, several of which feature sexy Vikings. Dad gave a lot of her stuff away to charity shops without checking with me first, which kind of sucked at the time and continues to kind of suck, but at least I have the brawny and imaginary arms of the sexy Vikings to comfort me in my hour of need.

# BOYS I LIKE (5, 3)

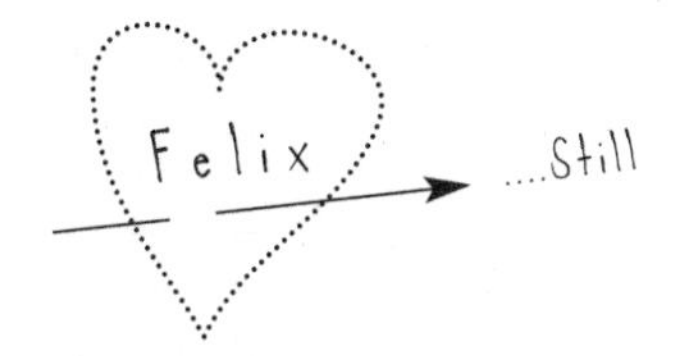


I know it is silly and pointless and that he is two years older than me and that that is a big deal at our age and that he is cooler than me and has more friends than I do. But it is hard to stop liking him when I see him every day after school. He is in TY this year, so he has loads of free time to faff around the house being unconventionally attractive. I say unconventionally because Ciara doesn't see it AT ALL, and she is usually quick to find someone to be cute. Joel doesn't see it either and I assume Ella wouldn't, seeing as how he is her brother.

I have liked him for over six months now and am learning to live with it, just as I would learn to live with disability or something. I now can form coherent sentences around Felix and sometimes even disagree with things that he says. Also his band, The Deep Tinkers, kind of suck, but the fact that he is in a band at all is amazing to me. I want to become their manager and make them rich enough to keep me in the manner to which my father has long been accustomed but I amn't really accustomed to at all. Only problem is, as I've said before, they do kind of suck.

Mac

I do not know a lot about Laura the Human Dolphin's boyfriend Mac, but what I do know is extremely good looking. I still can't decide if he looks more like a vampire or a fallen angel. Something from the cover of a book in the Dark Romance section of a bookshop, anyway. His eyebrows sweep up, so he always looks a bit surprised, his cheekbones could cut paper, and he has a thin upper lip and a big fat pillowy lower lip. His shoulders are broad, and he is quite tall and slim.

He wears nice clothes. And he has a ridiculously perfect girlfriend, which makes him even more unattainable. He often wears a battered leather jacket that used to belong to his father.

The way Laura said that made me think that his father was dead or something. I didn't ask, because I didn't want to appear nosy, but that might explain the sexily troubled look that occasionally passes over his porcelain features. Also it would mean we have a tragedy in common, which might lead to me being the only one who understands him which might lead to him breaking up with Laura to spend all his time hanging out with me, making snarky comments on the fringe of social gatherings like a hero. I have seen him four times now.

I still prefer Felix, though, because anyone with a pulse would fancy Mac, but Felix is an acquired taste particular to me, like that mouldy cheese Dad buys from the expensive cheesemongers down the road and which he appears to enjoy even though it tastes like powdered gym socks.

Liking people is weird. It happens so rarely. You'd think that being built the way we are and being so pumped up on hormones that everyone would be attracted to almost everyone else. But it doesn't work that way at all. I mean, it's kind of unusual for me to meet a boy that makes me wibble at the mere thought of him. I suppose that is a blessing in a way, as otherwise my life would be hampered by constant think-wibbling.

Mum had boyfriends, and sometimes – not often, mind – she would have what I now think were one-night stands. It is hard living in close proximity to someone – our place was really small: two bedrooms, a bathroom and a big sitting/kitchen/everything-else room. So we were close. We couldn't hide very much from each other and it is still strange to me sometimes how much SPACE there is in Fintan's house. *Our* house, I suppose it is now. It feels like home, but when I think of the other place, that feels like home as well.

We were renting – there are probably some other people living there now and they won't know about all the stuff we had: pictures and our big fat teapot that got broken on the way to Fintan's. I kept the lid. It is in the biscuit tin that serves as my safe. I like my biscuit tin. It says KEEP OUT: MAY CONTAIN BISCUITS on it in big black letters and for some reason that always makes me smile.

At the moment it contains a Deep Tinkers flyer, a page with some scribbled song lyrics, some cinema tickets, a concert ticket on a lanyard from that time Joel, Ciara and I went to the charity gig thing, a half empty bottle of Mum's perfume, half of one of Dad's novelty ties and some photos of me and Mum and Dad from when I was younger. Things I like to hang on to and remember. Beads from an old necklace, a flower from Mum's grave I picked and pressed.

**TY:** Short for transition year, which is the year between Junior Cert and fifth year. It is kind of a doss year, being more focused on field trips and work experience than exams and homework, but Felix seems to be enjoying it. I'm not sure if I'd like to do TY or not, because I started out secondary school wanting to go to college ASAP, and I suppose I still do, but I can kind of stand living with Fintan a lot better now, so TY is kind of an option.

Joel wants to do it, Ciara wants to skip it, but who cares because we won't have to decide for almost two years. Also, if I were to skip it, I would be in fifth year while Felix was in Leaving Cert, which would make us closer in school years, if not in actual age years. Which is an interesting point to note.

**UNCONVENTIONALLY ATTRACTIVE:** Handsome, but not the kind of handsome where you'd describe it to a person and they'd be all, 'This dude sounds handsome.' But if you showed them the person they'd be all, 'Oh, now I get it.' So, hot but not in a cookie-cutter, same-as-all-the-other-hot-people kind of way. Again, an acquired taste, like Fintan's stupid cheeses.

**COHERENT:** Something that makes sense, is easy to understand and clear in its meaning. Not the way I speak around boys I am attracted to.

**AMN'T:** Hiberno-English for 'am not'.

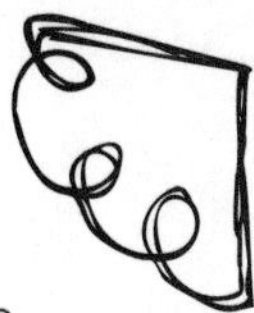

**UNATTAINABLE:** Ungettable. Something that cannot be gotten. To Roderick, this might be an appealingly nibble-able book-cover. To me, well ... there are a lot of things I want that are unattainable.

**PORCELAIN:** China, a fine, pale, delicate ceramic material. Usually expensive. May sometimes be used to describe the complexion of certain unattainable and conventionally attractive persons.

**IN CLOSE PROXIMITY TO:** Near, beside, close to. I would like to be in close proximity to Mac or Felix. Or even both, crushed between them in some sort of cosy, hair-gel-smelling boy sandwich. God, that sounds a bit pervy doesn't it? I wouldn't want to, like, have a threesome with them or anything. Just a fully clothed, chaste cuddle. Or a nap, like the way puppies sleep in videos on YouTube. That would be amazing. But the kind of amazing where you don't tell anyone you would like it to happen, ever, for fear they will not understand and get all judgemental and irritating.

**RODERICK:** My rat and the one member of my family I can trust to always be there for me. Mostly because I keep him in a cage. He has rakish whiskers and a fondness for being scratched behind the ears.

## DO OR ___ (FOLICALLY SPEAKING) (3)

The idea came to me in geography. Joel and Ciara hate the sound of what I am planning to do to my hair but that doesn't matter because Fintan lets me get my hair done any way I want now. (He calls it 'picking your battles'. I call it 'being the boss of what grows on my head'.)

We were talking about V-shaped valleys and I was gazing out of the window, wondering how many of us would ever need to use that information ever again. I reckon maybe two out of thirty, which isn't so bad, but still, I had the idea that I would probably not be one of them. Leona might, because she was wearing earrings made of geodes, which could denote an interest in rock formations. But then again, they are kind of lovely and I would like a pair, so not really indicative of anything beyond an enhanced ability to accessorise.

Joel was over the other side of the room. We are only allowed to sit beside each other in science and civics now because we find each other endlessly amusing and sometimes make up little songs and hum in the middle of class.

Anyway, I was looking at this tree, which had that lovely thing of sunlight filtering through leaves going on, pale green and dark green and glowy green and white, and all of a sudden this jackdaw alighted on a branch opposite me. I knew he was a jackdaw because we had a teacher in third class who was OBSESSED with birds to, like, an unhealthy degree, which means that all the kids in his class ended up being able to tell a jackdaw from a crow or a raven. I have only ever seen a raven once, but it was pretty cool. Anyway, whatever way the light was shining on his feathers, it made them look so black and sleek that they were shining green and purple as well in the magic light of the sun-tree.

**GEODE:** A stone that is cut open to reveal all these little crystal clusters inside it. It looks like something out of a fairy tale. How do people know what rocks to cut open? I think that a geode starts out as a normal rock and then a process happens and it becomes all magical and sparkly inside.

This is what Ciara thinks sex does to people. Not that she is having any of it, but she has, on occasion, alluded to worlds opening up and being a proper woman and fireworks and so on and so forth. I think it is my fault for lending her that book about the Viking and the stolen princess who becomes his servant and ultimately his bride. That Viking, Alfric, was a lot like a geode, as I recall. He was all rough and warrior-like on the outside, but on the inside he was full of manly vulnerability and tender glances. I wonder where I could get a pair of geode earrings?

And I decided I was going to dye my hair the same colour as that jackdaw in the light, because it was just so lovely and nature-y and made me think about how intricate and magical the world is, how many little entities there are, going about their business, no matter what is happening in our stupid human lives.

No sooner had I made that decision than I was asked a question about glaciers, which I got right because, as I told the teacher when she asked me why I was looking out the window, 'I use my eyes for looking and my ears for listening.'

She sent me to Ms Cleary's office and Karen was all 'good enough for you'. I genuinely didn't mean to be rude or anything, though, I just wasn't thinking clearly. About anything except hair. Ms Cleary was pretty cool, just told me to pull my socks up and stay out of trouble.

Also I have detention on Friday, which will be alright, I think, because it's only for two hours after school and it's not like there's anything good on. Anyway, my Saturday cheer-up plan of plans is to go get my hair dyed jackdaw. Because for that level of amazing, I will need the skills of a professional, at least at first.

This is only the second time I have had detention this year so that's not actually that bad. The first time was for rowing with Karen (again). I hate that girl; she's so full of bile and horror. She says things just to hurt people. I think she plans them, probably at night-time instead of doing homework. I hate her so much.

Sometimes I have to express my hatred by yelling at her when she does something particularly heinous. Teachers should understand this, and I know whenever anyone gets in trouble they always say that someone else started it, but Karen genuinely started it and deserved everything she got. Urrrrgh.

I think my new hair will look OK. Ciara says I will look like a 'punk rocker'. I have never met a 'punk rocker', but it seems like an awfully granddad-ish way to describe a person. If she is not careful, she will soon be taking up fishing and telling long pointless stories that don't go anywhere at all.

She kind of has the second one down already, though. Her and Syzmon do things and she tells me all about them in the minutest detail. Not physical stuff, obviously. But if they go to the cinema, for example, she will tell me what he wore and what she wore and how their respective hairs were done and what the film was about and what snacks they bought. And then she will expect me to remember it all. She does little quizzes throughout the day – not full-on ones like school tests or anything, but little jokey references that I won't get unless I have been listening carefully to her stories. I think she thinks that if she doesn't tell somebody about it, it is like it didn't happen.

I wonder would I be that way if I had a boyfriend? I do not think so. But maybe ... I keep my crushes close to my chest because I don't want them to be discussed as if they were, like, a thing, when they kind of only exist in my head. I would be seriously embarrassed if someone were to find out about them. And by someone, I mean either Felix or Mac. Or, heaven forbid, Laura the Human Dolphin. That would suck enormously.

# DYE

Ciara's grandmother is called Lily and she has moved into their granny flat. A granny flat is a little houseen off the corner of your house that you use to make extra money or put grannies in.

Mum and I lived in a granny flat for a year when I was eight. It was nice, but my bedroom was the sitting room, so I had to fold away my bed every morning, which was a bit annoying. I really looked forward to visiting Dad that year, I remember, because I had a big double bed in his house, and it felt HUGE compared to the sofa bed. Also, he never woke me up to look for keys or lipstick that had fallen between the sofa cushions, because my bed there had a proper mattress.

It wasn't that Mum didn't want the best for me, but money was tight and she didn't like taking it off Dad because then it was like he was paying her to have me and she got a bit squicked out by that idea.

'Squicked out' is a thing that Ciara says and now I have started to say it too. Isn't it bizarre how that happens sometimes? You, like, appropriate your friends' little quirks and turns of phrase, sucking them in until they are a part of who you are as well and you don't even think about them any more.

Granny Lily is really sick and can't make dinners or drive herself places any more. Also, she forgets things. It's not dementia, but it still means that it is safer for her to move out of her own little house and into Ciara's, where her family can keep an eye on her.

She is Ciara's dad's mum. Ciara's mum's mum died when Ciara was three. I wonder if Ciara's mum is jealous of Ciara's dad because his mum is alive and hers isn't. I am sometimes jealous of Joel and Ciara because they both have mums and I don't. Not that I get angry at them or anything, but sometimes I'll get this nasty little you-don't-know-how-lucky-you-are fist in my stomach. I don't like it because I know that if people had their way my mum would be alive and also I know for a fact that I don't want their mums to die, especially if Joel's mum, Anne, keeps baking scones with various unexpected fruits in them (blueberries, raspberries, pomegranate and passionfruit) and I get to eat the benefits. But still. I suppose it is like new-top envy only on a deeper, more feelingsy level.

And I know I have Fintan and he is great, in his own crap way. But it isn't the same as when Mum was alive, because I could talk to her about anything and she wouldn't judge me and she helped me with my homework, even when I didn't need it, which could be kind of annoying because sometimes I'd feel that I'd get it done quicker on my own. Fintan has never, ever offered to help me with my homework because he is never around when I do it.

I know there are things that he is better at than Mum was too, like being able to make loads of money. Also he is better at dating Hedda than Mum. Not that Mum dated Hedda, but Dad seems to be doing a pretty good job at that recently: they look all happy and interested in each other and she calls over more often than she used to. He can't call over to her house very often because of having to be a half decent father to me and stuff.

I wonder what it would be like if they got married. They would perhaps have pretty (Hedda), big-nosed (Fintan) children and that would be weird. I don't know if I would like a little half-brother or -sister. I have been an only child all my life. On the upside, though, Hedda hasn't had kids up until now, so maybe she doesn't want them.

Also Fintan is really busy, so a baby would probably be left to me a lot. And I do not have a good history in the whole 'being left alone with babies' department. Although the thrill of putting false moustaches on them has sort of worn off, mostly because of that time Joel used his theatrical make-up kit to put a full beard on his brother Marcus and it looked really realistic and amazing but somehow wrong, and we caught each other's eyes and said 'too far' and only took, like, five or six photos of the poor small fellow before abandoning the project.

Marcus has had to put up with a LOT, now that I come to think of it. He'll probably grow up to be either a saint or a master-criminal.

**APPROPRIATE:** Get, obtain, by fair means or foul. Not to be confused with *appropriate*, which is spelled the same way but pronounced 'a-pro-pree-it' and means suitable. As in, my hair was not deemed appropriate for school, so I appropriated the principal's golden retriever and held it to ransom. (I would never do that in real life. Pets are sacred.)

**HOUSEEN:** Like a house, only smaller. In the same way a girleen is a small girl or a careen is a small car. Mum and I used to have a careen at one time. Which is why I find the first name Carina weirdly hilarious.

# IT MAKES WOMEN DECIDE WHETHER OR NOT TO BE HONEST (8)

Big News. Dad asked Hedda to marry him.

Bigger News. And she turned him down.

I know I shouldn't laugh but, oh, this is priceless. Maybe just a giggle or two?

Ha. Ha-ha. Hahaha. Hahahahahahahahahahahahahahahahahahahahahahahaha.

Poor Dad.

It *is* funny, though.

They might be moving in together as well. But they have to iron out the details of it.

## PROPOSAL

Who does she think she is? My dad is too good for her. Or something. I am trying to be loyal because he is kind of upset. He keeps whining and demanding cups of tea. It's not like she broke up with him or anything.

Question-popping-wise, Dad was very cute about it. He took her to her favourite painting in the national gallery and proposed there, very quietly passing her the ring. I am so glad that I shared my thoughts on restaurant proposals with him, because it would have been horrible for her to turn him down with so many people around.

Luckily, they were by themselves in a room, because her favourite painting is that meeting-on-the-turret-stairs one that you can only see at limited times. Dad is a wily fox and let them know what he was at, so they gave him and Hedda some space. He had a little speech about how happy being with her made him and so on and so forth. I hope someone makes a complimentary little speech like that at me some day.

Anyway, Hedda was completely pole-axed by the proposal and the ring and whatnot, and she was very nice about it, saying that it was a huge decision and one that

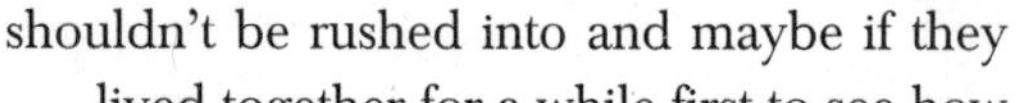

shouldn't be rushed into and maybe if they lived together for a while first to see how they suited?

She LOVED the ring, though. She told him it was perfect for her and made her want to say yes just so she could keep it. Poor Dad followed this with an extremely pathetic and hopeful, 'Why don't you, then?' This is the thing he

**POLE-AXED:** Stunned. A pole-axe is actually a type of weapon that basically looks just like an axe on top of a pole. If you got one to the gut, imagine how stunned you would feel!

regrets most about the whole debacle. Why did he say that? he wonders, as he analyses it over and over like some sort of slow-motion action replay of things that make him feel like a loser.

No woman has ever made him feel as needy as Hedda does. It is discomfiting.

I can't believe she said no. This does not play into the story of Dad's life at all. He has always done really well at almost everything he wanted to do well at. Except for soccer, which he loves but can only play adequately. Also, women were always trying to get him to marry them up till now. Even Mum had a bash at it when she first found out she was with child. Mainly so her parents would throw less of a hissy fit, but still.

Dad is used to being the rejecter, not the rejected. He did offer to marry Mum, but then they both thought better of it and decided to row almost constantly instead. Until I was born, anyway.

It will be weird, having my dad's girlfriend live here. I assume she will live here, because it is bigger, and her house would not have room for me and my rat as well as my dad.

I wonder if I am part of the reason she turned him down? I mean, being a stepmother is a big ask. She'd have to 'parent' me and stuff. Go to parent-teacher meetings. Pick me up from school. Make me dinners and wash my dirty socks. Not, like, all the time. But if she was

**DISCOMFITING:** Uncomfortable-making, unsettling. The time I accidentally walked in on Fintan trying on my eyeliner was extremely discomfiting and I told him so in no uncertain terms.

going to marry Dad, she would kind of be marrying me as well, at least until I go to college and move out. So, three to four years and then holidays – wow, that's actually soon. I am growing up fast. I can't wait to be in college. It looks like so much fun – you get to pick what you study and you have free time and there's always stuff going on.

Dad hasn't even noticed my new hair.

It is lovely, by the way. I went into the salon with the nicest sign (that's how I pick them) and booked an appointment with a man called Steve. Steve was six-foot-something tall and had one of those gauged ear piercings. I wanted to ask if he would let me put my finger through it, but that would have been weird. Like, unacceptably weird. Our conversation went like this.

**STEVE:** So, cut and colour — what do you have in mind?

**ME:** I want to get rid of the split ends, but keep most of the length if possible.

**STEVE:** OK.

**ME:** And I want the colour to be a really dark black with green and purply bits in, like the wing of a jackdaw in the sunlight that filters through the trees.

**STEVE:** I know exactly what you mean.

Then I put on a cape and went to the neck-hole sink, and an hour and a half later I looked the exact way I had imagined looking in my head when the jackdaw idea came to mind. Only a little shorter. Perhaps I should get some high-heeled boots?

## A DESTRUCTIVE MEAL (9)

At breakfast today, Fintan gazed at me in a bleary-eyed manner and asked me, 'What have you done to your hair?'

'Cut and colour, Fintan.'

'Call me Dad. It looks amazing.'

'I know, like a jackdaw on my head only sleek.'

Then he made me give him the name of the salon so he could go there. I hope he does not get the same hair-style as me. Hedda would never marry him then.

## BREAKFAST

School is a place that is full of rules. Stupid silly ones about what hair you can and cannot have. Joel and Ciara love my hair and admit that they were wrong. Ciara still thinks I look like a punk rocker, but she said it in a different tone of voice, like it was now a good thing to be.

Anyway, apparently my new hair colour is 'not natural', according to the powers that be. It is a damn sight more natural than the hair of Ms McBride, who has hair as bleached as butter and eyebrows as dark as if they were drawn on with sticks of charcoal. Not natural. I mean, really. What could be more natural then the fabulously dusky plumage of one of our native birds? Nothing. That's what. Stupid henna-purple Karen laughed at me when I got removed from class. How come she can have whatever hair she wants? People are always running after me with bushels, trying to put my light out. I am worried that Dad is going to kill me – he does not like having to leave work in the middle of the day at the best of times.

# THINGS THAT DID NOT

Ms McBride did not get over herself, even when instructed to do so by my beloved father in his deepest and most stroppy of tones.

I did not dye my hair back to its natural colour. Because that would be quitting. And quitting is something that a Hamilton never does, according to my father, who took up the zither after a holiday in Croatia three years ago.

I did not ask Fintan where his zither is, if he is such a not-quitter. Because he was on my side and I intended to keep it that way.

I refrained from pointing out that my surname is actually Leary, like Mum, as opposed to Hamilton, like Dad, while we were in the principal's office with Ms McBride, who is also deputy head and did most of, if not all, the talking. I did point it out after we left, though. Because if I hadn't I would have felt like I'd been dissing my dead mother. And rule number one of being someone's child is that you don't diss them after they have passed away. Unless it is really, really funny.

I did not get suspended, although threats were made.

I I did not point out how ridiculous it was that this is the thing that gets me into trouble. I mean, *this*. Last year, I punched another human being in the face and did not even get suspended or anything. Granted, it was Karen, so I was not entirely wrong, but how in the name of all that is holy is what I have done now worse than what I did then? OK, what I did then was in defence of Ella, whereas this is kind of just a celebration of my own vanity. So there's that. But my hair isn't hurting anyone, unless it is in the sense that it sometimes hurts the eye to look on things of terrible beauty, like the craggily wondrous Connemara mountains or the face of a benevolent god.

I did not have to listen to my dad whining on and on about being rejected. I did have to listen to him deciding to join the parents' committee, because changes need to be made. Stuff needs to be sown and then reaped. Stuff like tolerance of all creeds and religions, piercings and hairstyles. Only not the piercings, because facial ones creep Dad out to an appalling degree. He cannot look at them without imagining little pieces of food seeping out through them or clogging up the holes.

I did not get to go to Ella's and see my beloved Felix. But he did text me to say:

> Ella tells me you've been accused of having rebellious hair. Fight the Power, Leary. Fight the Power.

Isn't that sweet? He totally wants to have my babies. If only he knew I was mind-cheating on my secret crush on him with my secret crush on Mac. He would be SO nonplussed if he knew. Or maybe he would be scared and appalled.

Hedda did not call Dad. Because she is having space. Dad wanted me to text her to let her know about my hair thing, and also I was to put a question in so she would have to reply to it and we could analyse her reply and its impact on the future of FinHed. Nobody calls them FinHed, but I might start to because it is hilarious. I refused to send her the text because she wants space to think about moving in, and we mustn't remind her of the madcap schemes and political struggles that living with a scamp like me will involve. I did text Sorrel, though. She was very proud of me.

My geography homework did not get done, because I am not pleased with the way that I have been treated by the system. Until the system changes, no geography homework will be done.

**ZITHER:** An instrument that people in Croatia play, I assume. It has strings and frets, like a guitar, but does not have a neck. It is kind of straight on one side and curved on the other side. It is not easy to play, because it has about forty strings and stuff, but apparently it makes a lovely sound if you know how to play it.

Fintan does not know how to play his zither. He prefers to play his guitar, because he is actually pretty OK at that. It is a nice-looking thing, though, and it is a pity that he hardly ever uses it because I bet it cost a pretty penny.

**BENEVOLENT:** A kind of twinkly and enormous kindness, like new-testament God or childhood Santa. Benevolent people often give stuff away to the poor and needy.

**NONPLUSSED:** Surprised and confused but in a way that means you do nothing and are just all, 'Meh, I don't care'. Felix would be surprised to know I like him, but I do not think it would make a big difference to him one way or another. It is my thing and it doesn't really impact on him at all, no matter how much I would like it to, or imagine it does in silly little daydreams where I play the zither for the Deep Tinkers and earn his love and respect by my wondrous mastery at manipulating its thirty-eight strings to make a melodious and resonant sound. He would not fall in love with me, though. Even if I could play the zither and had a nicer forehead.

# A BIT OF A MASTER (11)

I told Fintan about my not doing my geography homework protest idea and he made me do my geography homework. My hand is tired from drawing diagrams of physical features.

Also, Joel rang. He walked in on his mum and dad kissing and murmuring sweet nothings in the kitchen.

'It was the most disgusting thing I have ever seen, Primrose. He completely finds her attractive and stuff. I almost got sick.'

'I am sorry you had to see that, Joel. But Anne is a sexy lady and your dad has totally done it with her at least twice.'

'STOP! She's my mum.'

'What? I'm totally right.'

'No.'

'Yes, and I can't say I blame him. If I were a man, I'd totally want to –'

'PRIMROSE!'

'Sorry.'

'Too far. I don't want them to split up or anything but there's nothing wrong with a chaste, pure sort of love that involves sharing chocolate with each other on a park bench when they are both old and grey.'

'Like in the ad.'

'Like in the ad. I love that ad.'

'I know. So cute.'

'Anyway, this has to stop. I will not put up with parents who kiss each other on the neck in kitchens.'

'On the NECK? That is dreadful. Social services might take Marcus off them.'

'I know. Being exposed to that sort of carry-on can't be good for him.'

'If only he had an Internet romance to take his mind off the whole sorry thing.'

'No. That was a bad idea.'

'It was funny, though, Joel.'

'That it was. Will you help me mow the lawn later?'

'Hmmm ...'

'Come on, Prim. You have LOADS of time on your hands now that you're being expelled.'

'I am so not being expelled – it's only hair, for crying out loud.'

'Karen says you're being expelled.'

'Ugh. I hate Karen. Why did you even listen to her?'

'Sinéad told Ciara and Ciara told me. I didn't really believe it, but Primrose?'

'Yes?'

'If you ever get expelled, promise that you'll text me about it.'

'I am *not* going to get expelled, Joel. But I will help you mow the lawn.'

And so I did. It wasn't too hard anyway. They have one of those little tractor-shaped mowers that you drive around the garden on. It is red and cute and has a little beepy horn you toot for people to get out of your way. The only annoying bit is emptying the grass baskets when you finish. It makes your hands all dirty and green.

But I did end up promising that I will not be grossed out by Anne and Liam showing each other affection. I suppose all the years of Mum's boyfriends and Dad's girlfriends made me invulnerable to disgust of that nature.

Besides, Anne is only lovely and deserves to be treated like a queen. She has been so kind to me since I was small. Liam too. Joel has been spoilt by their happy normality and only appreciates them sometimes, like when they get him a present or something.

I can't believe Karen told everyone I was expelled. I hate that girl so much that steam comes out my ears whenever I think about her, as though I were a particularly angry cartoon rabbit.

**INVULNERABLE:** Un-wound-able. Not easily hurt. Wolverine is nigh invulnerable and I think Superman is as well. The difference is that Wolverine isn't smug about it and that is why I prefer him. I am invulnerable to some things, but other times I feel like I am the opposite of invulnerable, like I'm made of fontanelles or something.

**FONTANELLE:** The little hollow that newborn babies have on the tops of their heads where the skulls haven't fully grown over the brain yet. They feel like the softest velvet in the world and smell of newborn baby. Rubbing them almost makes me cry because of how fragile and vulnerable they feel and how scary and big and full of dangerous things the world is.

# MASTERPIECE

I am not changing my hair. EVER. Turns out Steve-who-does-hair is Ms Cleary's (first name Fatima, which always delights me, because it is so unexpected and kind of exotic) nephew. He rang the house yesterday because he wanted me to drop in a photo of my hair to put in his portfolio. I told him that my hair might be short-lived because of the powers that be at school. He made the connection and rang his auntie Fatima to tell her that there is no way that she can destroy his masterpiece. I am his masterpiece.

I am going back to school tomorrow with a fine head of hair. Dad will not have to sue everyone like he threatened to do. Happy endings for all concerned.

Dad was a little creeped-out that a grown man rang the house asking for a picture of his teenage daughter, but has cheered up considerably since and is watching the match and chuckling with triumph at having won his war with the school uniform policy. Even though he didn't really. Steve did. But it still counts as a victory.

I am so pleased with myself right now. I have let Roderick scuttle around my room while I do a dance of

> **MASTERPIECE:** The best thing you've ever done. In a job sense. Like, let's say Leonardo da Vinci gave his life to save that of a child. Well, although that might be his most noble act, his masterpiece would still be the *Mona Lisa*. I prefer the one with the lady holding a ferret, though, because it reminds me of my small rat man and how happy he makes me.

triumph to music that is turned up really loud. My dance of triumph is a lot like all my other dances, except that it involves a lot of air-punching. And leg-kicking. I think I may be terrifying poor Roderick. He is hiding behind my CD cases and only peering out sometimes.

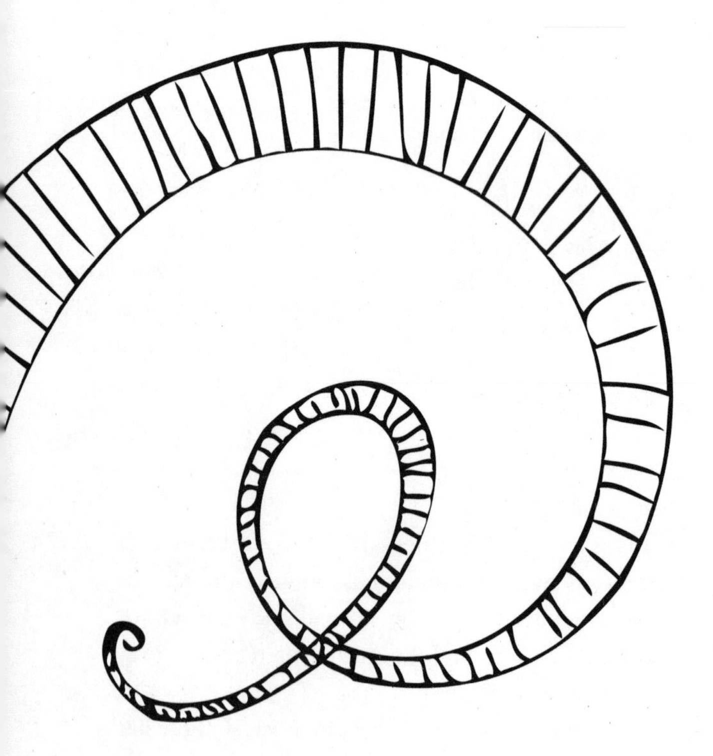

## REASONS USED TO BE PLANS (12)

There was a half-eaten bag of crisps behind my CD cases. Me and my rat are both triumphant now. Yes indeed.

## EXPLANATIONS

I went into town with Joel and Ella. I texted Ciara but she didn't want to come with us. She was going somewhere with her family or something. We went for tea and then to the pharmacist's. Joel is thinking about dyeing his hair because he is a big copy-cat. He didn't like any of the men's hair colours and wouldn't consider buying any of the ladies' dyes, which is silly because it is just hair dye – I mean, it's not like the chemical make-up of it is any different based on the gender of the grower of the hair. But whatever.

We spent a lot of time in the big pet shop too. Ella wanted to get some stuff for Mr Cat and I needed to get Roderick some food and a new hammock because his old one is all nibbled and wobbly.

While I was looking at the rats (there were some new baby ones, all curious and snuggly, so cute), Caleb came over and said, 'Hi.' He was looking at the rats as well. I said, 'Hi' back, but I was trying to be non-committal. Joel and Ella were upstairs looking at the snakes but I wished that they would come down because I have not been very comfortable around Caleb since the time he spat on me after I hit Karen, back when they were going out.

He said, 'You have a pet rat, don't you?' And I said, 'Yeah' because I was holding a bag that said 'rat food' and any other answer would have seemed a bit insane, and went up to join the others, even though I don't like looking at the snakes and lizards because some of them eat mice and rats and there is a sad-making doom-fridge up there, filled to the brim with furry little corpses, that disturbs me greatly.

I do not think that Caleb should be allowed to get a rat, seeing as he is a bully. Also, he is mercurial. Because he and Karen used to be joined at the lip, but now they hardly even acknowledge each other at all. I assume this means that they have broken up. Which is good, because they are both the Devil and do not deserve to be in a happy boy–girl relationship when I (who am not the Devil) must content myself with impossible crushes and melancholy daydreams set to a power-pop soundtrack.

Anyway, after we left the pet shop, we talked about how rotten Karen and, by extension, Caleb were, and how it was never OK to spit on someone. Ella kindly pointed out that it was also never OK to punch someone in the face, but that was different, because

a) I was defending Ella's good name,

b) it wasn't much of a punch and

c) Karen is the Devil, and I think it is OK to fight the Devil.

Ella got annoyed about my whole insistence that Karen is the Devil because she does not believe in the

Devil, and even if she did she would not think Karen is he or she. It is a bit implausible. But we did both agree that Karen is a nasty piece of work. (That is what Mary, Ella's mum, calls people who are mean.)

I know by the way Joel's been acting recently (shaving regularly even though he doesn't need to, buying those stupid little weights) that he would really like to meet someone special. I know he would. He sings along with sappy love songs on the radio as if he means them and I think he daydreams just as much as I do. He just hasn't told me about who yet. And I know the reason why and he knows I know, so I don't understand what the big deal is with saying it out loud.

Anyway, that is up to him and is also none of my business. Except I want him to be happy, so it kind of is. I mean, there is nothing wrong with being attracted to boys instead of girls. And I know he thinks there'll be all this drama and whatnot if he actually admits it to people but I really don't think there will be. And if there is, it'll totally pass because anyone who knows Joel loves him to bits. He is all warm and funny and strong and likeable and people are just drawn to him, like moths to a lovely, friendly, not-going-to-burn-you flame.

I wish that there was something I could do to make it easier. I think that the stuff he went through in his last school really dented his confidence, even though to look at him you wouldn't know it. He had to move from St John of God's to my school because he was being bullied there. He still won't call it 'bullying' either. I think that he thinks that in some way he deserved it or brought it on himself or something. And that breaks my heart.

**MERCURIAL:** Changeable, unpredictable. Like how sometimes sour cola bottles are my absolute favourite type of sweet, but at others only the delicious small fried eggs will assuage my sweet hunger. Also, how sometimes I love Ciara to bits but other times I'm all eye-rolly and 'for God's sake' at her. I am pretty mercurial. I would like to be less so.

**ACKNOWLEDGE:** Admit or accept that something is the case, or that you know something or someone. Like if Joel came into the room and was all 'Howya?' I would acknowledge him with either a theatrical wink, indicating that I was in flying form or a surly 'Grand', indicating that things could be better but I did not want to talk about it.

**MELANCHOLY:** Like sadness, only prettier.

**SCANDALISED:** Shocked! Appalled! Outraged! Taken aback! Probably by some form of scandalous behaviour. Like hardcore parent-on-parent neck-kissing action.

**MR CAT:** Ella's cat, which we got from a shelter last year. He is a very grumpy individual but has been known to show affection when there is some sort of food-like treat involved. He has very long whiskers and a sort of cat-version of a beard, where the fur on his chin is longer than the fur on the rest of his head. It looks very dignified indeed. Sometimes Mr Cat has been known to be dressed in teeny tiny women's clothes. This usually results in glowering of the highest order.

## A WEEK LONG AGO (1, 8)

Last night Dad was a bit weird and distant and stuff. Then this morning he sat me down and said he had something to tell me. I swear to God, I thought he had cancer or something, from the tone of his voice, and I was almost physically shaking because I can't go through what happened with Mum again, only a lot slower and without any spare parent to fall back on. I literally do not know what would happen to me if Dad were to get sick. But it kind of surprised me that that was the first thing that came to mind, because I hadn't really worried about it up till now.

Anyway, what he had to tell me was less life-shatteringly dreadful, but still seems so terribly, terribly unfair. Brian McAllister has been released from prison, less than a year and a half after he got sentenced to three years for killing my mother with his car while he was drunk.

I don't know how to feel about that. I mean, initially I was relieved that Dad wasn't sick, but then the suckiness of it all sank in. I mean, the reason Dad found out is that he (Brian McA) applied for a job at Dad's friend's firm. It wasn't like the police rang us up and told us or anything.

> **IRREVERSIBLY:**
> Unchangeably. If something is irreversible, it can't be undone or righted. You just have to cope with it.

You'd think they would have done. You'd think there'd be a law where they would have to. I mean, he took my mother's life. His actions changed my life irreversibly. And there he is, applying for jobs, like he was a normal person. Like he deserves a job. There are plenty of people who haven't killed anyone looking for work at the moment, without letting him loose with a CV and a motor-car. I don't think he is allowed to drive for a long time, though. But who knows? I mean, he was supposed to be in prison.

My head is going in so many circles. I can't concentrate on anything. I just keep falling back into this chicken–eggy loop of crime and punishment and what is and isn't fair.

I am worried about school tomorrow. Dad says I have to go because it is not like Brian McAllister will be there or anything. Which is true, but in a sense he will be. Because he is out in the world and so am I. We could, like, bump into each other in town.

**HYPOTHETICAL:** Theoretical, imaginary. Good for playing out scenarios in your head. I once asked Ciara, 'What would you do if Syzmon cheated on you?' and she replied, without a flicker of emotion, 'Then I would kill him.' I am pretty sure she was joking, but I am very glad that the scenario was a hypothetical one. Although, if it came to it, I would probably give her an alibi. I like Ciara a lot.

I wonder would he recognise my face? I think I'd know him, but I amn't sure: I didn't exactly spend the day of the hearing glaring at him and memorising his features.

Dad was wondering whether or not to tell me, and he decided it was better that I find out from him than some other way, like the aforementioned hypothetical town-bumping. That is the thing with prison sentences: unless you have done something very bold indeed, you can get out earlier than you are supposed to 'on good behaviour'. No matter that a thirty-two-year-old woman is dead because of you. Agh. It makes me really frustrated.

**AN UNBIASED OUTSIDER:** Someone who has nothing to do with the situation and would therefore think about it objectively. Kind of like 'a reasonable man' or 'a normal person'. It is hard to think like one of these when you are not actually one.

But then I remove myself from the situation and try to look at it as if I were an unbiased outsider. And I do believe that people should be forgiven and reintegrated back into society and things, I don't want him dead or anything but still ... it's just really, really hard to accept.

I am lying on my bed with Roderick snuggling his head into the crook of my armpit and I don't know what to do. The world is so big and people are so stupid and I am so utterly, utterly powerless. I wish Dad hadn't told me. But I'm glad he did. I don't think he would have this time last year. And this time two years ago, Mum would have been alive, so it wouldn't have been an issue.

We talked about it, Dad and I, for a while, but not too long because, even though my brain is overactive, there is not really all that much to say before you start repeating yourself. Angrily, and with hand gestures. Which never really solves anything. Thinking and moping are the best course of action for me now, I think. And I do those best alone, except for my Roderick, who provides an ear and the warmth of a tiny hot-water bottle. He loves me unconditionally, like Mum did. Well, I suppose the only condition being that I don't, like, step on him or anything. Mum wouldn't have liked being stepped on either, except in some sort of weird yoga/massage context.

I wonder what she would have made of all this? I often find myself wondering that, but I can't really give myself a definite answer that isn't based on guesswork mixed with what I would want her to think. I mean, she isn't here, so I'll never really one-hundred-per-cent know how she would have reacted, whether she would have loved my hair or thought I was too young for it or something.

If Brian McAllister had only injured her, if she had had to go through almost two years of physio only to see him out on the streets again before she could even walk properly, before she could earn a living or whatever, would she have been angry? Because no matter how injured you are, it is almost always better than being dead, than not being anything at all any more.

I think she would have been angry. I think she would be so, so very angry if she knew that he was out walking the streets like it was over. Like her death was over. But it isn't. She will never not be dead and I hate this. I hate it so much. It makes me angry in a way I don't like. A sad, destructive, hating kind of anger is what it is and I am powerless in all of this and it's not even a small bit fair.

I wish I had more of a life, something to take my mind off all of this stuff that I can't control. I always feel like other people are more interesting than me, even though they can't ALL be. Or maybe they can?

I am just feeling that the world is a very unfair place right now. I mean, how can people do things like that and just get away with it? Not completely, I know, there is the guilt and stuff, but I don't think his guilt is going to be even one fraction of what I feel every day. I am still not used to not having a mum. And sometimes when I go a whole day without missing her or wishing she was here, I will get this huge wave of guilt about it, like my being happy when she's dead is a slap in the face to her or something.

I don't really talk about it, not since I stopped going to therapy. The group thing was fine but it didn't really make much of a difference to me one way or another. I think that if I'm going to be sad about something, I'm going to be sad about it, and there's not much that talking it out with a group of other sad people and one happy leader-type can do to change it.

I'm mostly OK, though. I think I'm coping well. Suppressing the urge to find out where B McA lives and burn it to the ground, but mostly OK.

I don't know if I want to be a cruciverbalist any more. Maybe I will be a vigilante instead. Or just someone with really good hair.

**VIGILANTE:** Basically a citizen who takes it upon himself or herself to uphold the law without being a part of state-sanctioned law enforcement. Like Batman, these people are generally a little bit mental. Unlike Batman, these people are generally not awesome and are rarely play-boy millionaires by day.

# A SENNIGHT

Ella went a bit funny today. Maugie's (her SNA's) hours have been cut this year – she's only with Ella for mornings now – and so she was all by herself, which kind of unsettles her.

She kept tapping and muttering and couldn't stop, even when Ms Smith gave out to her. Teachers rarely give out to Ella because it's kind of harder for her than it is for the rest of us. I don't know why Ms Smith was so snappy with her; it was really stupid and unproductive.

I offered to take Ella out for a breath of fresh air, because sometimes Maugie does that and it's not like being in class was doing her any good, but Ms Smith accused me of skiving off. As if. I never skive. (That isn't exactly true. I rarely skive. But I wouldn't use Ella as some sort of skiving aide. It wouldn't be fair: she's my friend, even if she can be a bit baffling at times.)

To be honest, I felt a bit muttery today myself. My muttering would have been a good deal swearier than Ella's, though. I am still kind of het up about the whole my-mother's-killer-being-out-on-the-streets thing. The same streets that people who haven't killed anyone can walk on. I couldn't switch my brain off. It just kept at me all day, like an alarm clock with no snooze button.

And I know this is going to sound really stupid and whatnot, but I was kind of jealous of Ella today, because she can get away with stuff that I can't, and people feel sorry for her when she's all het up, instead of calling her a grumpus.

Ciara called me a grumpus eight times today. She obviously heard the word somewhere over the weekend and was looking for an excuse to use it. Joel told me that I had a face like a smacked bottom, which was more hurtful, and also not true at all. I do not have round pink cheeks. When I pointed that out, he called me a grumpus and high-fived Ciara enthusiastically. I hate the two of them. They would turn even the nicest, cheeriest person into a grumpus. Which, as I pointed out to Ciara about seven times, is NOT EVEN A WORD.

Of course, I was shooting myself in the foot there. Because being pedantic about what is and is not a word is exactly the kind of thing a grumpus would do.

Also of course, they were both lovely to Ella. Which I don't resent or anything; I'm not completely self-centred. I mean, they probably would have been lovely to me as well if I'd told them about the whole Brian McAllister thing. I kind of don't know why I didn't tell them. Maybe because that would make it all more real? Or maybe I didn't want it turned into drama, which it kind of is already. I mean, my feelings about the whole thing are pretty dramatic, but you know the way once you mention a thing in school suddenly everyone knows and it's all this major gossip? I really didn't want that. If there is to be major gossip about me, I want it to be because I have successfully stolen Mac from Dolphin Laura and we are engaged to be teenage-married. Not for stupid hurtful reasons that I don't like talking or thinking or hearing about.

After school, Ella wanted to be by herself. She was really frustrated and just went into her room with Mr Cat.

I did my homework in the kitchen. I took a break halfway through to help Mary peel potatoes. When her back was turned my hand slipped and I sliced off a couple of layers of thumb-skin. There was a fair amount of blood on the peelings but none on the actual potatoes. Mary put disinfectant and a bandage on my thumb. The bandage had Winnie the Pooh on it for some reason. It must have been quite old – Felix and Ella are kind of past the Winnie the Pooh stage. Also, Ella hates Winnie the Pooh, because his name is disgusting to her.

I'm not sure if my hand slipping was on purpose or not. Is that weird? I was kind of thinking about what would happen if the peeler sliced my thumb and then before I knew it, it was happening. I was letting it happen, and it's like nothing else counts when you are concentrating on that, which can sometimes be kind of a relief, if you see what I mean?

Of course, now my thumb hurts like nobody's business and I still have geography, French and science to finish off.

Also Roderick finds my thumb bandage mysteriously delicious. He keeps on licking it and trying to eat around the edges. He is doing himself no favours by conforming to the rats-liking-to-nibble-disgusting-things stereotype. Next thing I know, he'll be spreading plague in the fourteenth century. I'm tired. I might just leave it. What is the worst that could happen?

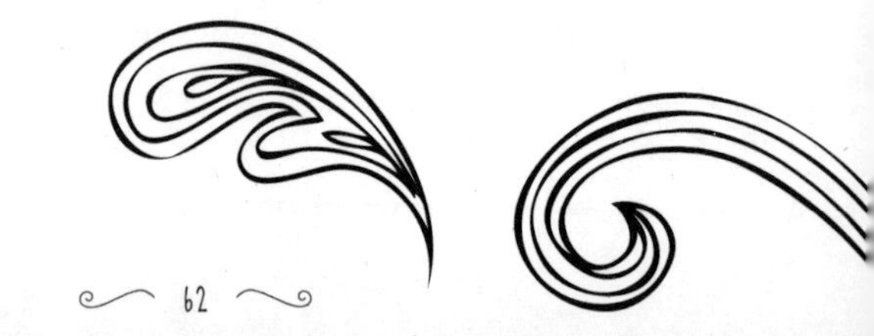

# ROUNDED 14TH-CENTURY SWELLINGS SOUNDING SAUCY (6)

When I didn't do my homework I forgot one thing: how much I hate being picked on by teachers. I kind of like sailing along, being one of the clever ones, only ever getting negative attention for messing with my friends. And last night it seemed like it would be OK. That I would just put up with it and that the extra hour of bad television and listening to Dad grumbling about his un-ironed shirts (our cleaning lady is on holidays) would be worth the nagging.

I actually even ironed four of his shirts and three of his trousers. He pretends that he isn't able to do it, but he is well able. He just doesn't like it. It is kind of the same way I feel about mopping floors. God, I hate mopping floors. I'm glad I never have to do that in this house, although I do sometimes help Anne or Mary out with it the odd time. Mum hated it too. (You see – I get that from her.) So we'd always argue over whose turn it was to do it.

Anyway, when I waltzed in to school this morning after my extremely wonderful night of hardcore ironing fun-time, I got this weird feeling in my stomach, you know the muffin bit that pokes out when your jeans get too small for you? That exact bit of my stomach was full of a tension heaviness that seemed to whisper to me 'Primrose ...'

'What, very specific section of my stomach?'

'Primrose ...'

'Stop being mysterious and tell me what you want.'

'You don't have to go to school today, Primrose.'

'Stop saying my name, belly-part. And don't be ridiculous, of course I have to go to school today. I'm wearing my uniform and everything.'

'You have maths first class and you haven't done your homework.'

'Fair point. But I should still probably go in.'

'It is a sunny morning, you have half a Kit-Kat and a paperback about murderous monks in your school-bag.'

'I'm listening ...'

And listen I did, until I found that my stomach had convinced me to take the morning off. I snuggled up beside a particularly mossy tombstone in the graveyard near our school, munching and reading away as if I had not a care in the world. It was only marvellous. Not that I'll be doing it all the time, mind. But once in a while couldn't hurt much. It put me in a good mood for the day, actually.

And I didn't tell anyone that I hadn't had a dentist's appointment. Even Joel. It is good to have some secrets because it makes you feel powerful, like not everyone knows all there is to know about you.

**ROSARY:** Basically a whole lot of prayers that you say using beads. You have to do one prayer for every bead and repeat as required, depending on how much you want to get into heaven.

Ciara was in a bad mood today. It is like we are all taking turns. It is not easy living with Lily. She is very set in her ways and makes Ciara say the rosary with her every night. And not just a decade of the rosary. The entire thing from start to finish. Ciara is getting increasingly frustrated with it, but she can't exactly back out because no one else is going to do it. Her mum doesn't have the patience and her dad is always working. It is enough to make her want to eat her own hair again, like she used to do in primary school. I can tell because her nails are all picked and bitten down.

Ciara likes Lily but she doesn't really know her – they only saw her once every couple of weeks before she moved in – and it is weird, having a new member of the family living in the house. Lily doesn't really boss her around or anything, but she likes to watch TV in the family room and that means Ciara can't watch what she likes.

Ciara doesn't really read much, not unless she really likes the book she's reading, but she does like television. She thinks that book about the sexy knights would make a good film. I don't know if it would, because there was just so much to it, all battles and poultices and kidnappings and girls dressing up as boys to learn sword-fighting and then knights thinking that they are attracted to a young boy when in reality it is just a girl with short hair and whatever the medieval version of a minimiser bra was.

**POULTICE:** A kind of dressing featuring herbs and spices and ingredients. Ladies that Vikings end up marrying use it to dress their Viking wounds. The application of a soothing poultice to a wound is often used as an excuse for some serious chest-ogling and -stroking in the romance novels about fighting men from the past.

Anyway, Ciara can't go on saying the rosary every night. She just can't. It is making her tired and grumpy and also weirdly anachronistic. She says old lady things now, like 'Jesus, Mary and Joseph' and 'Lord bless us and save us and protect us from all harm' and 'Look at the cut of you.' Joel and I find this amusing and endearing but we are worried that we will start doing it too. Which wouldn't be very nice at all. Although I wouldn't mind saying the rosary once or twice, just so I know how it goes. I might need it to get into heaven.

Oh, God, what if that actually ends up being true? If it is, Mum is definitely not in heaven. But she wouldn't be in hell either because she was lovely. Lovely people don't go to hell.

Although, different people have different perceptions of what is and isn't lovely. Karen probably thinks that she is lovely. Except she couldn't possibly think that if she has even a modicum of self-awareness, seeing as how she revels in being evil incarnate. She told me my shoes were fugly today. My shoes are not fugly. Not that they are super-pretty, mind. They are inoffensive black ballet flats that never did a thing to harm anyone. I bought them because I read in a magazine about this thing called a capsule wardrobe,

**ANACHRONISTIC:** Old-timey, but in the modern world. Something that doesn't belong to the time in which it is found. Like a Viking who finds himself transported to modern-day Manhattan by a magical love-mist, only to unexpectedly encounter a hotshot female reporter who will teach him to love something other than longboats and elaborate helmets. The anachronism there would be the Viking.

where you have only about seven different pieces of clothing (not including tights and underwear) but together they make about seven thousand different outfits, like those Japanese robots that slot into each other to become one much bigger, super effective robot.

Marcus, Joel's little brother, thinks that robots are magnificent. I concur, but I do not insist that every item of clothing I own has some sort of robot on it. Joel had to order some robot patches online and sew them to Marcus's jeans and T-shirts so that they would become acceptable apparel for his little brother. I kind of admire Marcus's attitude. I hope he never changes and that he becomes rich and famous enough that his quirk is found enchanting and original, as opposed to extremely unsettling.

I am staying over at Joel's on Friday night. We are babysitting Marcus while Anne and Liam go for a romantic meal. Love is in the air for people who are too old to deserve it any more, apparently, because Hedda and Dad are going out too, I think.

Hedda hasn't been around in a while. I hope she doesn't dump Dad for wanting to marry her but being confused about how her 'moving in together' idea would work. I think she is cooking for him in her house. I have never been to Hedda's house. Dad says it is very nice but quite small. I don't think there would be space for all our stuff there. So a-babysitting I will go.

I like babysitting because small children are silly and fun, but it can be a lot of work as well. So much can go wrong. Like when they start to cry instead of going to bed and you can't peacefully enjoy late-night television but instead have to cheer them up by reading, like, ten bedtime stories and doing all the voices until your throat is sore from growling like a Gruffalo and squeaking like a mouse. Marcus isn't really like that, though, because Joel can give out to him and stuff.

Also there is generally delicious food in the cupboards because Anne is still baking away like some sort of TV chef. Liam goes on work trips a lot so Joel and Marcus and I generally get to eat the lion's share of this baking, and that's a good thing. My favourite so far were her raspberry and white chocolate muffins. I could eat those muffins for breakfast, dinner and tea. Actually, I'll go further than that. It would be my honour to eat as many of those muffins as she can possibly bake. They are *that* good.

I went to swimming after school today, which means I have to do all my homework now. I felt like it was such a bother when I was getting my stuff together and changing and whatever, but once I was in the water it was like I could put everything out of my mind, all the clamouring, and just go back and forth, thrashing and gasping, kicking and breathing and holding my breath and going for it and not stopping until the teacher blew her whistle and told us what to do next.

Butterfly is the best for angry water-displacement, all that flapping, but my favourite is the breast-stroke, not because of its sexy connotations but because to my childlike mind it is the way that mermaids swim, hair floating out like seaweed behind them. It can be slow or fast, but it is neat and drifty and something about it makes my body feel almost graceful. I rarely feel graceful because I am always dropping things and having mishaps. Like that thing with the peeler yesterday. My thumb is still stinging. The bandage came off in the water, floating grossly to the bottom to infect the pool until it has been cleaned. I was too busy swimming to dive down and get it. I didn't want to interrupt the class. Dolphin Laura could probably bob up and down in seconds if it was her bandage. I cannot, though.

Laura's mum was picking her up today. Mac couldn't do it because he had to go somewhere with his dad.

It just came out: 'I thought his dad was dead.'

She said she didn't know why I would think that. I didn't know myself, just something in her voice when she mentioned him before: a change in tone. A pausing or uncertainty. There was a little wobble in her voice when she said, 'No, he's back with them and everything is fine now.'

I said, 'I didn't mean to be nosy.'

'You weren't. It's just a weird situation.'

'None of my business.'

'Not that – well, kind of that, but not in a mean way. It's just ... it's his stuff, not mine to tell. I wouldn't feel comfortable.'

'I get it.'

We were brushing our hair in the mirror and after I said that I left. She stayed to blow-dry her hair. I like to do mine at home because the hairdryers at the pool are always either too hot or too cold and there is the tiny but unmistakable risk of death by electrocution. I saw that safety DVD about hairdryers and bathtubs when we were in primary school and it seems like it could easily be applied to swimming pools as well. You can't be too careful.

Poor Mac. His sexily troubled hotness is more than just a façade. I wonder what the story is with his dad. Perhaps I could console him through whatever it is in a friend-with-benefits type way. A friend-with-benefits is a friend who you get to do it with but you're not going out with them or anything. It is one of those relationship deals that would be amazing for one member of the relationship (the member that liked doing it with their friend but also with other people) but not so good for the other member (the one that secretly fancies their friend and hopes that the benefits accrued will one day include marriage). This is what I have learned from things I saw on telly.

I would like to be Mac's friend-with-benefits. He would be completely smitten with me but I would be holding out for Felix and therefore irresistible. Dolphin Laura would soon be forgotten when he saw how unavailable I was. I would only text him when I wanted to hook up, and our chemistry would build and build until we fell in love in spite of ourselves. And also in spite of Dolphin Laura. In my fantasy, she and Mac aren't going out, though. I don't want to hurt anyone's feelings. Except for possibly my own.

## BUBOES

Joel and I had a lot of fun minding Marcus. We made him a robot costume out of cardboard boxes and tin foil. He was well pleased.

Ciara was going to call over for a bit but then Syzmon wanted to go to the cinema or something, so she did that instead. I was kind of relieved, actually. I love Ciara to bits but she is always around and since Joel is in our school now I feel like I get to spend less time with him by himself than before.

Joel is really easy-going and sociable, unlike grumpy, snarky me, which is part of why we get on so well. But he is happy out in big groups, whereas I feel like I do myself more justice when it's just me and one other person, like I can be nicer and friendlier and funnier when I can give them my undivided attention and not worry about leaving anyone out or having anyone think I'm an idiot or something. Not that Ciara has ever called me an idiot, but there is some stuff that Joel and I like that she doesn't really get.

Like putting false moustaches on babies. She told me she never really 'got' that. (How?) Of course, she waited till we kind of stopped doing it very often at all to say anything. Ciara likes to blend in – like if Joel and I started smoking, she totally would too, even though she is really precious about her nails and hair. Not that smoking does anything to your hair apart from make it smell of smoke.

It's not a bad thing, being the way Ciara is. It means she can get on with almost anyone, but sometimes I wonder how well I really know her, how much of her is being what she thinks I would like her to be, like laughing at my jokes even when she doesn't really get them, or helping us put mutton chops and a full, bristly Victorian-style 'tache on Marcus even when she doesn't 'get' it. I think that was why she hung around with Karen and them for so long, even when they were being really mean to her. She just wanted to be liked.

Her mum puts her under a lot of pressure. One time when I was over at her house, she was finishing her homework and I was reading a magazine because I can learn things off a lot faster than she can, and her mum came in and gave out to her for slacking off, because if she had been working hard she would have finished at the same time as me, which isn't even logical. Our brains are different. She is better at doing neat handwriting and making things look lovely, and I am better at racing through dates and facts and vomiting them back out again in tests. Her mum always asks her who did better than her in tests, even when she gets an A.

Another reason I was glad Ciara wasn't around was that it soon became clear that Joel had something to tell me. He was all cagey, but in a noticeable way, like he wanted me to grill him about whatever he was hiding, because he was dying to tell someone. So I did what he wanted and asked him what was up. And after a cursory amount of pussyfooting around the place and grinning, he told me what was up.

And what it was was kind of huge. He told me he was pretty sure he was gay. Which I totally knew already, but just to hear him say it was enormous and I gave him a hug and said that I kind of guessed that already, but I was so proud of him for being strong enough to say it out loud. And then he dropped the bombshell. The reason he has become so sure of his sexual identity is because he has a big old crush on someone. Which is a good thing, because it made him more confident about himself, but also a bad thing, because how do you know if someone else is gay or not? It is not like they come with some sort of special mark or tattoo.

Joel is pretty sure that Kevin – that is the guy's name – is not gay, though. But they get on really well and have the same sense of humour and they both like martial arts. That is where they met: at Mixed Martial Arts.

So, Kevin is a little taller than Joel, with sandy brown hair and blue eyes. He's got quite a stocky frame and he dresses well, but not crazy well. Usually nice jeans and T-shirts. He wore a surfer-style necklace one week, but he hasn't worn it since, so Joel thinks maybe that Kevin thought that he couldn't pull it off even though he could, because he has a very nice neck. Kevin likes very loud rock music and has a Jack Russell named Wayne Rooney. He didn't name it, though; his little sister did. Wayne Rooney goes missing a lot and various members of their family have to walk around calling his name loudly. Wayne Rooney will not answer to Wayne, or Rooney, or Dog, or Boy. He will only respond to his full name and this irritates Kevin, who is convinced that the dog is trying to humiliate him on some deep level.

Also, Joel and he are going for coffee after Mixed Martial Arts tomorrow, but it isn't like a date or anything, because Kevin isn't gay, but wouldn't it be great if he were?

I will be so jealous if Joel gets a boyfriend before me. I know that he deserves to find love as much as the next person, but if a gay fifteen-year-old who has no intention of telling anyone but me that he is gay can get a boyfriend and I, a heterosexual girl of average attractiveness except for my hair, which is shinily wondrous, am left all on my own, I will feel so left out. I know I will. Even as I was conspiring with Joel about how to woo the dashing Kevin in a purely-platonic-but-whatever-happens-happens way, I was worrying about being the only one in the group apart from Ella with nobody to hold hands with.

Actually, I wonder if Ella will ever be able to have a relationship? I think she totally will, but it would have to be with someone patient and understanding and with a deep love of anecdotes about her cat. I've never talked to her about boys, really. I mean, she's been around me and Ciara while we talked about Syzmon or whoever, and I assume she knows about my shameful crush on her brother by the way I turn into a stammering tomato-face whenever he enters a room, but she's never really volunteered her own ideas about this whole love business.

It must make things difficult for her, the Asperger's. I mean, I find it hard to relate to people and get on with them a lot of the time and I'm supposedly normal. Joel is five thousand times more normal and likeable than me and yet I'm sworn to secrecy about a significant chunk of who he really is. He thinks his parents would freak out if they knew. I'd say they have to have some idea, but then again adults are pretty dense, so it is hard to say what they do or do not guess.

I told Joel we needed to celebrate his coming out in a symbolic manner, so we went down to the kitchen. There was red wine in the fridge, which is gross, but I filled two glasses a quarter full of it and we toasted being ourselves and being happy that way. Then I furtively washed the glasses out, feeling slightly guilty about the whole thing. Liam, Anne and Fintan are so lucky. I mean, we are ridiculously sensible as fourteen-year-olds go: no smoking, no drinking (or almost none), no drugs or sex or anything else you hear about on those radio shows where people ring in to complain about what kids these days get up to.

Also, we put on some old Hallowe'en masks and snuck into the closet in Marcus's room. We leapt out at him with fabulous growls of doom and terror. He was very unimpressed. He has become inured to our torments, having had to deal with being treated as a sort of living dress-up doll by us from such a young age. He went back to sleep almost right away. I sometimes wonder at how delighted I still am by childish things like dressing up and being stupidly funny. I don't know if I'll ever grow out of it, but I probably will. Or at least become a little bit more reserved.

Anne and Liam did not return home until half past three in the morning. Joel and I were still up chatting but once we saw the lights of the taxi we scuttled off to bed. I couldn't fall asleep for ages and ages, though. I really, really hope everything turns out OK for Joel. I want him to be happy, even if that means that he gets a boyfriend before me, starts spending all his time with him and semi-abandons me except when they're rowing. That is how much I value his friendship.

I wish I had a picture of Mac to show him, but I can't find him on any of the social networking sites. Possibly because I have yet to find out his full name. Which could one day be my name too, if he breaks up with Dolphin Laura and realises that what he needed was here, right here all along. Well, not exactly here, as in close to him, but here as in somewhere in the general vicinity of him for about three minutes once a week or so.

I also told Joel about Brian McAllister and he got all mad at me for not saying anything earlier, but not really mad, just kind of pretend mad – like, frustrated.

'You never tell me anything' was one of the things he said. And I told him I didn't want to talk about it at school because I knew I would probably start to cry and it would be like this whole big thing with Ciara flapping and people looking and Ella becoming irritated by my big red wobbly face and gasping noises.

'That's why phones were invented, Prim.'

'I know. But I just don't like talking about it.'

'You should, though, because you're not in therapy any more.'

'Thank God.'

'I know, but it means that you have to tell people about stuff, not bottle it all up to rant to Triona once a week.'

(Triona used to be my counsellor but I hated her and I am never going back to her.)

'But talking about my stuff is boring. And it's not like saying things out loud makes them disappear.'

'I take back being gay, then.'

'Don't be stupid. That's totally different.'

'It's still bottling, Prim, just in a different bottle.'

'I told you about liking Mac, though.'

'You tell everyone about liking Mac. You'd get a tattoo of his face on your face if you could.'

'No I wouldn't.' (Maybe on my ribcage?)

'Yes, you would – but it is easier to talk about normal things, like boys, than it is to talk about things that make you different, like tragedy and sexuality and so on.'

'You are right.'

'I am always right.'

'No, you aren't. Remember when you wanted to grow a moustache so you could be cool, like my dad?'

'I was only six or something.'

'You were eleven, Joel.'

'I still do want to grow a moustache some day. Just to prove that I can.'

'Me too.'

'No you don't.'

'You're probably right.'

Joel is very wise sometimes. I did have a bit of a cry, in bed by myself, quietly, so as not to wake Marcus, who I have to share with. He heard me, though, and got up and rubbed his hand all over my face and said, 'No crying for robots. Beep-beep.'

And I said, 'Beep-beep, Marcus. Robot Prim feels better now.'

'Beep-beep, Prim.'

'Beep-beep, Marcus.'
'Beep-beep. I. Am. A. Robot.'

'Beep-beep. I. know.'

'Beep-beep. I. Love. You. Goodnight kisses.'

And he slobbered all over my face and snuggled in beside me. He smelled of Plasticine and that children's toothpaste that tastes of strawberry Mr Freezes and not mint. Anne found us like that in the morning and was all 'Aw'. Which is kind of a double standard because she always gives out when Joel and I end up in bed together.

I like Robot Marcus a lot. Maybe he could be my new counsellor. We could just go for cuddle-naps once a week and have long, beepy talks together about a variety of issues. At least that way Dad's money would be well-spent on robot paraphernalia and sweets that look like robot food.

I kind of love Joel's family. Even Liam, who thinks I am dafter than a brush made of March hares, mainly because I turned his son into a robot by sticking false moustaches on him and showing him the film Wall-E. I wonder if he'll think I turned Joel gay by sticking false moustaches on him and being his best friend? Eep.

## BOYS AND BIRDS (5)

Dad picked me up on Saturday morning and we went for a walk on the pier and by the harbour. There were gulls and things, swooping and pecking. Seagulls look really evil – they have a cruel, sneery aspect to their beaks which makes me think of a flock of arrogant Karens. Shudder.

Dad was in bad form because Hedda and he are trying to iron out the details of moving in together, and the logistics are kind of baffling. She is reluctant to give up her house, and it wouldn't be feasible for us to move in with her. They considered getting a new house, a neutral space for the three of us, but then decided that it seemed like an awful lot of effort. So Hedda is going to try living with us for two weeks starting next weekend, and we'll see how that goes. Poor Dad. Nothing is ever simple.

She's going to stay in his room, obviously enough, so we had to clear out one of his wardrobes. It was full of clothes he doesn't wear and stuff he doesn't use – exercise equipment, old band T-shirts and a portable record player and some vinyl records from back in the day.

It wasn't too difficult to sort out the wardrobe because everything was boxed and labelled and stacked already. Dad is nothing if not scarily organised and incredibly lazy about household tasks. The stuff had been boxed since we moved in the summer before last. I asked if I could take the record player up to my room until he finds the best place for it and he said yes.

Silly Fintan. He will never find the best place for it because he forgets about stuff he cannot see unless it has to do with work. It is mine now until I want to get rid of it. He showed me how to work it and move from track to track. It is more fiddly than a CD player, which is itself more fiddly than just playing tracks on iTunes, but I kind of like putting a bit more effort in. Plus, you can see it going around and around and around and around.

I had a sudden urge to put Roderick on top of one to see what would happen but Fintan said that would be a bad idea, as his little claws would scratch the records and they are precious relics from his youth that need to be handled with the utmost care. So we took the record off

**LOGISTICS**: The co-ordination or organisation of something. How you get stuff done.

**FEASIBLE**: Do-able, but not in the way that Mac is do-able. I think about Mac too much. It really is a problem. Pretend I said realistic instead.

and put Roderick on the turntable. He only went around and around once before he jumped off in disgust. Fintan wanted to put him back on and get the camera but I refused to allow it. My rat has his dignity, dammit.

So, it was a lovely, lazy Saturday. I even let the old fella pick the film we watched in the evening as we chowed down on deli-bought roast chicken, various salads and fresh bread with melty, melty butter.

I spent a good part of the day wondering how Joel's not-date with Kevin went. It turns out that it did not go at all: Kevin cancelled on him. I texted Joel to suggest that Kevin was treating him mean to keep him keen, but all I got in reply was a very ambiguous smiley face – the one with sunglasses and a neutral expression. What did it mean? I could not work it out, nor could I get through to him on his mobile or landline. Perhaps, instead of drinking coffee, they have run away together like the Famous Five. Or like Romeo and Juliet tried to do. I hope not. I would miss the hell out of Joel were he gone.

I did my homework while listening to one of Dad's old jazz records. It had a man smoking on the cover in black and white, so I knew it was going to be cool as all get out. Too cool for school-work. The kind of cool that makes Dad squint his eyes and tap his feet and click his fingers and be of the opinion that he is some sort of awesome lounge lizard, when in reality he is just a sad old number-cruncher whose girlfriend won't marry him. That was mean. But parents can't be cool. When will they learn that? I'd send out a massive group email to all the parents I know, only Fintan and his moustache would get all bristlily irate with me and probably not let me do things that I like doing. He's not a bad father, though, just kind of an embarrassing one every now and then.

At ten o'clock, when I was lying in bed thinking and waiting to fall asleep, I realised it had almost been a day and a half since I'd thought about you-know-who.

Which is kind of amazing, but also it made me wonder if I was being unfair to Mum.

## GULLS

Today was kind of a mess. Joel avoided me most of the day so we wouldn't have to talk about the text he sent me last night that told me to forget what he had said, that it didn't mean anything, he had changed his mind. I rang him after that but he didn't answer his phone.

Dad and I visited Mum's grave yesterday. We do that once a week because it is important to me.

I don't know what I need to do to change the way I am. I'm full of worries. The scabs on my legs from where I cut myself while shaving glue my tights to my skin. I have to tear myself to peel them off. I feel itchy and dirty and wrong. Something is happening to me. And I don't know how to make it stop. My head is moving so quickly even when my body is still.

I forgot my locker key today. I was so close to punching the door, which I know would do no good but might at least ease a bit of my frustration, when Caleb came up behind me with a pair of bolt cutters. He keeps them on hand, apparently; wouldn't say why. We snapped the lock off and he lent me his one for the day, because no one would go near his locker anyway due to his well-earned reputation as the kind of boy who spits on his enemies. It was weirdly nice of him. Maybe he is coming down with a touch of humanity?

I bought a new lock at lunchtime. I walked to the little shop fifteen minutes away that sells everything. It might be where Caleb got his bolt cutters, come to think of it. When I came back, Ciara and Ella were huffy with me for not telling them where I had been. They were sitting with Lauren and them and didn't even say hello. Joel did say hello, but it was a 'Shut your face if you know what's good for you' sort of hello. The kind of hello I can do without.

Caleb's hands were covered in tiny little scars, the size of grains of rice, some red, some white, some purple. I wonder what is wrong with him – on many levels, but the hand thing kind of sparked my interest. I didn't ask, though, for fear he would break into my locker and fill it with an assortment of nightmares.

My hands are small and kind of pinkly wrinkled on the palms. My nails are a little bit longer than they were. Scratching itches has become more satisfying now.

Mum's grave didn't feel like a visit to a real person. It felt like an admonishment. Like it should matter more, should be this big symbolic thing. But she is gone, and graves are made of earth and plants and stones. Sometimes my brain lets me make her grave into something more than that, but yesterday it didn't and I felt like screaming because I really needed comfort. I really needed Mum to be there for me and she wasn't.

Because she's dead. You can't be mad at somebody for dying. I mean, you can't. It isn't fair on them. But still ... that's how I felt. Or something.

Leona wasn't wearing her geode earrings today but she did say that they're going to this tacky teenage club event thing on Friday night. Ciara wants to go. She was on about it on the phone tonight. I might go, if Joel does too. And Ella. Although Ella mightn't like it if it's loud and full of people sweating and jostling.

What do people wear to these things? Would a band t-shirt, a floopy canary-coloured skirt and my slip on runners be OK? Or do I have to put something a good deal sluttier on? Like a sparkly hot-pant unitard and some sort of stiletto-type affair? I do not own a sparkly hot-pant unitard but if I end up wearing one I think I will want to wear fairy wings with it – my ones I wore last Hallowe'en to Syzmon's party are still on top of the wardrobe. I made them out of gardening wire, gauze and tights, and had to take them off halfway through the night and leave them in the hall.

My legs feel all prickly again. They don't look too bad, but when I run my hands down them they're all spiky and gross. I don't know if they'll ever get smooth, no matter how often or how roughly I shave them or how zealously I apply fancy moisturisers that smell like things I haven't ever eaten.

**ADMONISHMENT:** A gentle but unmistakable giving-outty-ness. Ciara is very good at admonishing me. 'Those shoes?' she says, tilting her head to one side in a manner that screams

'NOT THOSE SHOES FOR THE LOVE OF ALL THAT'S HOLY'.

She does not need to raise her voice or say anything more. I will take off my giraffe-print sequined wedges with the lime-green beading that I got for ten euro in a closing down sale. Someday I will find the perfect outfit for them. And then she will eat her admonishy words.

**UNITARD:** Like a leotard, but it goes right down to your knees or ankles or higher up than that in the tantalising case of the hot-pant unitard. Another word for it would be body-stocking. I like the word body-stocking, because it sounds kind of filthy. Especially if you say it in the voice of a British earl: 'Oh, I say. I must commend you on your body-stocking. Good show.' Earls like to say 'good show' when I am being them.

**ZEALOUSLY:** This does not mean 'jealous with a z instead of j'. Do not be fooled! It means eagerly. As in, I zealously applied the tanning product to my legs, little knowing that my zeal would result in streaks of orange-tinted tragedy.

## SUNDAY IN IRAN (6)

Joel was in better form today. I told him very seriously that we needed to talk.

'No, Prim, we really, really don't.'

'Yes we do, or I will smack your stupid face, Joely-Bowly.'

I gave Caleb his lock back and thanked him for his very helpful bolt-cutting. It is important to thank people for doing you favours, even if they have spat on you in the past. This will encourage the favour-doing and discourage any future spitting. He mumbled something along the lines of, 'It's OK,' but as I turned to go, he called me back to ask me if I knew anything about ferrets.

'Ferrets?'

'Yeah.'

'Why would I know about ferrets?'

'Well ... you have a rat.' At this point, he did a big long sigh that spoke of frustrations a-plenty. 'See ... my brother got this ferret and it kept biting him, so he was going to drown it and so I said I'd take it, but it keeps biting me all over my hands. Look.'

At this point he showed me all the scars I'd noticed on his hands.

'They look sore. Um, rats and ferrets aren't very similar, but I think I might know someone who used to have one. I'll give him a call tonight and see.'

'Your boyfriend?'

'No! God, no. He's Mum's age.'

I am pleased that someone thinks I am capable of having a boyfriend. I may have misjudged Caleb – he seems to be a lot more helpful and not-spitty this calendar year.

The person I was thinking of ringing was Mum's ex, Dave, who gave me Roderick. Since we met him, he has had a boa constrictor, a chameleon, two geckos, a Russian hamster named Boris and a degu. He is bound to have had a ferret at some stage or know something about them anyway.

But then I remembered about Ella and her encyclopaedic knowledge of all things veterinary. So I asked her what Caleb should do. She said that ferrets sleep fourteen to eighteen hours a day, so he should be safe for most of the time. It is important not to wake them up or surprise them while they are dozing. Also, if they hiss you should leave them alone. She was ready to say more but I thought it would be better to take her directly to Caleb.

So I did, and she held a small clinic, telling him that things like putting a horrible-tasting deterrent made of cider vinegar and lemon juice on his hands could work wonders, and encouraging

**DEGU:** If a rat and a squirrel had a baby, it would look like a degu. They are from South America and are very cute indeed and good at jumping. I wonder how I could convince Roderick to get a squirrel pregnant. I am getting ahead of myself. First things first: I wonder where I could find a promiscuous and not too picky squirrel ...

**DETERRENT:** Something that deters you from doing something. Like a slap or a small electric shock. Roderick is deterred from eating the skirting boards by being swiftly imprisoned in his cage as soon as he even looks sideways at one of the skirting boards. We do not want a repeat of what happened in my bedroom, where the skirting boards and chair legs are now nibbled to an alarming degree.

him to 'scruff and drag' the ferret to assert his dominance and let the ferret know who is the boss. Caleb said his brother Stan used to flick the ferret's nose whenever he was bold, which is apparently a combination of stupid, cruel and useless. Ella does not mince her words when it comes to pet-care.

Caleb seemed to know what she was talking about, though, and he even took notes. Ella said that he could ask her more questions if the ferret, whose name is Doctor Herringbone Dread after some DJ that Caleb's brother likes, is still giving trouble.

Caleb does not want to lose the Doctor, so he has been trying his best to toilet train him and make him a pet who does not bite everything. I hope he is successful. I know how much I love Roderick. I would hate to lose him for something that isn't his fault at all.

Ella thinks that Stan was probably abusive to the Doctor, and Caleb said he totally was. He used to try to make Doctor Herringbone Dread drink beer, and lift him up and swing him by one ferrety paw just to see the expression on his little furry face. Ella and I hate Stan now, even though we have never met him.

Also, kind of warming to Caleb. People who are kind to animals are generally decent. Except for Hitler, who was really nice to dogs, according to a documentary

**ASSERTING DOMINANCE:** Letting someone who is not the boss know who the boss is. Animals do this by growling and fighting. Humans do this by bossing people around and being allowed to get away with treating other humans like they do not matter.

Syzmon saw on the History Channel. Ciara, Syzmon and Joel were not very interested in Caleb's ferret, because none of them have pets of their own. But it was nice to have a lunch break where Ella got to do most of the talking for once. I like when she comes into her own and shows people how cool and clever and great she can be. She is going to make a kick-ass vet some day.

I think I am going to go to this thing on Friday. Ciara says I can come over to get ready and then stay at hers that night if I want. Could be really fun, provided she doesn't, like, try to put fake tan on me. I don't think she will, although she did once try to pluck my eyebrows while I was asleep. Apparently they were uneven. She apologised for it, but being woken up that way is not something you forget. Anyway, my eyebrows are fine. They are totally even. They don't exactly match my hair-colour, mind you, but it would be weird if they did. Imagine eyebrows with little bits of green and purple in them. That would be madness.

Also, Ciara has a surprise for me which she assured me was not an impromptu eyebrow-reshaping session. I like surprises, provided they are not unpleasant. I hope it is a cake of some description. Or the perfect pair of black floral lace-pattern tights. Long have I searched for the perfect pair of black floral lace-pattern tights, but to no avail. I have about eight pairs of reasonable black floral lace-pattern tights and I like them fine but something is missing. Something that turns cute into wonderful and 'They're nice' into 'I want to kill you so I can rip those tights off your dead body and have them for my own'. Someday I will own the black floral lace-pattern tights of my dreams. But until that day something will always be missing from my decidedly imperfect, pale, stubbly, leg-patterned legs. Sigh.

Anyway, I think I will wear my purple tutu and some sort of top to this thing on Friday. I have not worn my purple tutu yet because I vowed that the first time I wore it would involve dancing. Friday will involve dancing. Dancing and vow-fulfilment. Yay!!

## FRIDAY

I could start ranting now but I think that if I tell it like a story then it might put things into perspective, stop my over-emotional reaction and the waves of self-pity that led to snapping at Dad and Joel and Ciara and even poor smelly little Roderick who never did a thing to hurt anyone, unless they stood between him and a delicious treat of some description.

Friday night was like a graph. The graph started off suspicious, swiftly rising to good then swooping up to better before plateauing for a time at fun. It dipped almost imperceptibly later in the night when I got thirsty, but rose again for a time once I got a drink of water into me. Ultimately, however, it was to plummet to the depths of woe that change the way you view the world FOREVER.

And finally it rose a bit again, though what was learned at the bottom of the graph could never be unlearned. For, you see, no matter how long and mouldy and full of drunk-person-wee the tunnel might be, there is usually some light at the end of it. Even if it is the headlights of some oncoming traffic being driven by a flock of vodka-soaked killers with seriously impaired judgement.

I suppose I'll begin at the beginning. In the beginning, it was Friday. I had homework but it was mostly done and Dad was dropping me over to Ciara's house to get ready. He was going to the theatre with Hedda after and was in the kind of good mood that he gets when he is going to spend time with her. I wonder if it will last after she moves in. Constantly chipper Fintan would be hard to stomach, I think. I wish this was my biggest problem.

I was going to Ciara's house because this is the way of things before dancey-type events. Girls get ready in clusters so they can critique each other's looks and build up each other's fragile teenage self-esteem before going out into the wild.

Joel was there too, even though he is a boy and not a girl. He was there to play Xbox on Ciara's bedroom TV and complain about how shallow we were.

We were pretty shallow. There was a lot of earring- and bracelet-related talk. Did you know that if you wear a ring, a bracelet, a necklace and earrings all at once it can sometimes be overkill? Sometimes but not necessarily always. It depends on several factors: the positioning and adjacence of the bracelet and rings and the dimensions of the necklace – its statementitude, if you will. Ciara is a big fan of 'statement' jewellery. This is jewellery that says in a loud voice, 'I AM JEWELLERY.'

Grandma Lily prefers a more delicate, feminine chain. Also, she will only wear real gold or silver. No costume jewellery for her. It must all be real, and one day it will all be Ciara's. Grandma Lily enjoys Ciara's company and has grown to respect her more, because standing up for what you believe in is a very Grandma Lily trait and Ciara is doing this more often now that she has someone around to consistently back her up.

Lily was there not to help us get ready, but to keep an eye on us because Ciara's parents were out. This is why Joel was allowed in the room.

Ciara's parents are very strict about not having boys in her room. This is why she mostly goes to Syzmon's house when they want to hook up. Syzmon's parents are more lenient about such things. And although I can kind of understand (understand, not agree with) where Ciara's parents are coming from with the whole Syzmon thing, I don't get why Joel is not allowed either. I mean, there's no way anything would happen with Joel. Even if he was a fan of the ladies for all his sexy-time needs, he would not want to hook up with Ciara because she is very high-maintenance and demands teddies with hearts on them for Valentine's Day and other accoutrements like that. She is a girl who uses the term 'Weekiversary' without irony. Luckily, Syzmon is mad enough about her to be very assiduous about things like that, winning her things with claw machines, buying her cards with rhymes about the colours of various flowers in and so on and so forth.

Anyway, Joel should be allowed in Ciara's room, because he is her friend, not some massive sex-pervert who cannot be contained. I am more of a sex-pervert than he is and I'm hardly a pervert at all, though I do possess a long raincoat and unfettered Internet access.

Ciara was wearing a little black and lime-green pinstriped pencil skirt, a sleeveless and silky black top and heels of the sort that a promiscuous secretary would wear in an advert about sexy coffee. Also red lipstick. She looked great, very polished and wiggly. This was unsurprising, as she had been worrying about what to wear for what felt like weeks and weeks but was probably only about six or seven lunchtimes. I had my purple tutu, an old band T-shirt of Dad's for some dude called Rory Gallagher and my sequined black tennis shoes with the purple and black polka dot laces Joel had got me.

Ciara looked me up and down, said, 'Nice look – but give it to me for a second,' and proceeded to produce an ENORMOUS dressmaker's scissors and cut poor Fintan's T-shirt to shreds. I put on an old jumper of hers and we went down to Lily's flat and Ciara borrowed her sewing machine and did some stuff to the T-shirt that made it look a lot better on me than it had before. It clung in the right places and had some holes that looked a bit lacy or arty or something and when Joel saw me wearing it he went, 'Wow', and he does not say wow lightly.

I did not know Ciara was an amazing seamstress, but there you go. Lily said I should see her hats, but she wouldn't show them off because she has 'only recently taken up millinery and they're not ready to be shown to anyone yet'. I asked her if she knew how incredibly cool that was. I only wish I had an awesomely secret talent like that. I can touch my nose with my tongue but that is literally the only talent I have.

Anyway, Grandma Lily (who isn't supposed to be driving any more, except when Ciara's parents need her to be their little blue-haired chauffeuse) dropped us to the club where the

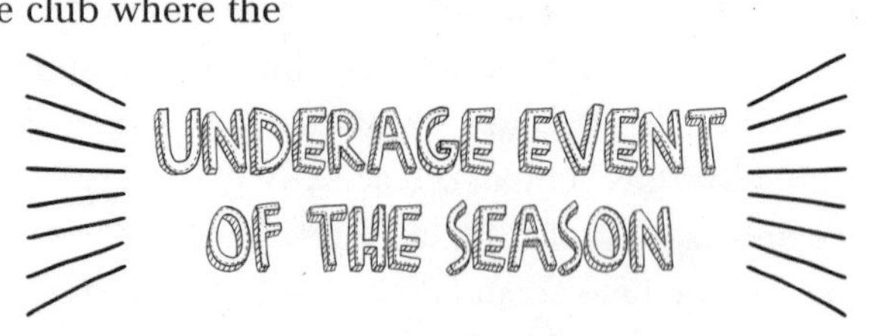


was on and loads of people we knew and knew by reputation were there. We spent most of our time in the queue to get in noticing people and saying hello.

I was surprised by how many people were drinking bottles of fizzy drinks while they waited and then copped that fizzy was not all that those drinks were. The scandal! I wondered if this dance thing would be on the radio the next day, like that one last year where loads of the girls didn't bother with underwear and scandalised the matrons of Dublin with their drunkenness and fondling. Because I was supposed to go to that one and then I couldn't at the last minute and after that chat show about it Fintan got really wound up and has ONLY NOW forgotten about it, even though I always wear underwear because I consider a warm bottom essential in our inclement Irish climate.

It's not like I'm against drinking or anything. I have been known to try a sip or two of the many weird bottles in Fintan's copious liquor cabinet when Joel is over and we feel like being bold. It just didn't occur to me to bring drink with me tonight, and also no one mentioned it and I kind of wouldn't want to be drinking unless Ciara and Joel were as well, because if we are going to be silly, it is WAY more fun to be collectively silly, as opposed to just one person being silly and the other two raining on her parade and making her feel like the biggest tool in the box.

Karen and them were all drinking of course, as were a fair few of the guys. But my tiny mind was soon distracted from all their antics by the advent of a big surprise. Caleb and Ella showed up together. She was all 'Hey' and cool, as if going to cramped places filled with loud noises was something she did every day.

She had been over visiting the Doctor. By which I mean the ferret. Ella is apparently very good with the Doctor. He likes to curl around her neck like some sort of fancy fur scarf worn by *grandes dames* of the theatre to premieres. Only alive and more bitey. She only has one ferret hickey, though. Apparently, after he'd tried it once, she gave him a stern look and a spritz of punishment spray and then the Doctor realised who the boss was.

Caleb's presence annoyed Karen and she gave our group a look of DEATH. Caleb wasn't sure why she was so annoyed, seeing as how they broke up because she cheated on him five times in one night because he refused to take her to see a romantic comedy about hairdressers in the Savoy.

When Ciara heard that, she called Karen a 'brazen strumpet', which made us all laugh because Ciara has really been spending far too much time with Lily. Ella asked what a 'brazen strumpet' was and Joel explained that it was 'old Person for whore'. Then I got all up on my high horse because I am my mother's daughter and my mother did not approve of such slurs. If a boy cheated on a girl five times in one night to prove a point, he would be a 'player' or at worst a 'bastard' (which is another slur that I hate because I am proud to have been 'born on the wrong side of the blanket', as Grandma Lily would put it, proud I tell you – shows my mum had sense).

Karen, although her behaviour could be construed as promiscuous, is not a slut, a whore, a ho-bag, a town bicycle (Lily again – do they do nothing but discuss euphemisms for this sort of thing?), a strumpet, a floozy, a tramp, a tart, a harlot, a scarlet woman (this one is my favourite as it sounds quite cool), a hussy and so on and so forth. We spent quite a bit of time coming up with all the words that Karen shouldn't be called, although it occurs to me now that if she heard us brainstorming she might not have gotten that I was defending her from slut-shaming because it is hard to compile a list like that collectively without getting the giggles. I shouldn't feel bad, though, because what she did to Caleb was very mean indeed. I wonder will I ever get the chance to be a scarlet woman? It could be fun, but only for a summer. I think a summer of scarlet abandon would be kind of amazing. Perhaps post-Junior-Cert?

Once we got in, after having our bags searched for contraband by three burly men and two burly ladies, the place was actually quite cool. There were a few people from primary school there who said, 'Heeey', and, 'Haven't seen you in aaages,' and other sentences with too many enthusiastic vowels in, and the music was really good, if a little bit on the poppy side.

Ciara wanted to dance right away but Joel and I were a bit shy so we all got lemonades instead. I kind of wanted to see who was there and what they were wearing and if I looked like an idiot compared to them. I didn't look like anyone there really, but I felt good. There were a lot of fake-tanned legs and tiny shiny dresses.

Leona was wearing a dress that looked like an old man's shirt with a waistcoat over it and loads of beads and mad earrings. She looked amazing and I told her so when she came over for a chat.

Joel's Kevin was there and he came over too, and so did Laura the Human Dolphin and Mac. All of a sudden, we were in the centre of this enormous group of friendly joking people and it was lovely. We all went out dancing and they didn't even seem to mind when myself and Ciara busted out sweet, sweet rap battle moves on the floor. This involves lots of swaying and dramatic hand gestures as well as a very tough expression on the face that says, 'Do not mess with me or I will cut you to the quick with my apt and insightful rhymes.' Laura joined in and she was very, very good at busting a move, for a Human Dolphin.

Joel and Kevin were talking and after a while Joel pulled me aside and was all, 'Oh my God, he has something to tell me! We're going to meet up tomorrow to talk!' and I was excited for him, but also worried because although Kevin looked like he was fond of Joel, there was nothing overly flirty or whatever in the way they interacted and ... Anyway, I hope it went well. Must call Joel later when I am ready to speak to other human beings again.

Song after song passed and it was amazing for ages, till it wasn't.

I got thirsty and got a tap water and then went back to dance and everything was fine until I needed to pee and Ciara couldn't come as well because Syzmon had arrived and they were busy kissing and doing the dance that isn't like a dance at all, just like a hug with swaying. So that was OK, but I wonder would things have been different if she had been there when I heard. I don't know. Maybe.

As I climbed the stairs to the bathroom, my phone beeped. It was Felix.

> Ella's missing. She left to go to the doctor eight hours ago and hasn't come back. Any clue where she mite be?

I still fancy him quite a bit, actually. I texted back to let him know she was here, and safe and happy. I didn't mention that the Doctor was a ferret because I did not want to blow his mind, unless it be in a more romantic and less rodenty manner. Oh, Felix.

I went into the bathroom and there was a huge queue of girls, some of whom were puking. I helped a girl called Charlotte retrieve and put on both of her shoes, which she had taken off in a fit of high-heeled agony, which abated after she stepped in something she was pretty sure had once been chips.

Felix rang while I was sitting on the loo, and I didn't answer because I make it a policy never to do so midstream. That time is mine and mine alone, and the Devil take the consequences!

When I got out, Karen was at the sinks, sneering at Siobhán who was sort of taking a nap on an out-of-order toilet (seat down, because she's not an animal). It is very hard to be the Devil without expertly applied eyeliner, so Karen applied some gel eyeliner from a pot with a little brush she had secreted somewhere on her person (I actually have no idea where she had it on her; she would do very well in prison) before turning to me with the smuggest expression that she has ever had. And this is a girl who, if she were a cat, would be constantly eating cream and also salmon.

'Primrose!!!' she said, in that really fake I'm-happy-to-see-you-but-really-I-amn't-wait-for-what-I'm-going-to-say-next-because-it'll-probably-haunt-you-for-decades kind of way. 'I'm surprised at you.'

I looked at her, like, 'What?' and then followed my look up with the actual question 'What?' because that was kind of where my look had been going but she hadn't answered me.

She pressed her lips together, in case someone's pet goldfish escaped her mouth, swallowed once and let it rip.

'Well, I didn't know you could be so ... forgiving.'

Again, I went, 'What?' but this time my voice must have had a bit more contempt in it, and also I had started drying my hands, so she couldn't really draw it out for fear I'd escape on her.

'I suppose it's hard for you to make friends. I mean ... well, that's why you hang out with the ... Ella.'

She literally thinks that Ella is not a real person, that she's somehow less than other people because she has Asperger's syndrome. I know Karen thinks that she is better than almost everyone including me (because I'm clever, which makes me a nerd, and I don't know as many people as she does, which makes me a loser), Ciara (because she used to eat her own hair, which makes her abnormal), Joel (because he is friends with me and I once punched her in the face) – the list goes on. But in Ella's case she really, REALLY thinks it, more than usual.

'But I thought ...' she was saying now, 'well. It seems a bit odd, like you don't really care that his dad smooshed your mum and stuff.'

# SMOOSHED?????

I'd like to get some driving lessons, take my driving test, pass my driving test, fill in a form, enclose money and two passport photographs, wait till my licence arrives in the post four to six weeks later, drink a bottle of vodka and smoosh the hell out of her.

But wait, there's more. And the more is why I was too stunned to punch her all over again.

'What do you mean?' Siobhán asked from the toilet seat, where she was blinking and focusing on the world outside the cubicle as though it were some sort of test she was in the process of trying desperately not to fail.

'Oh, just the thing I was telling you earlier – about how Primrose is all in love with Malcolm McAllister. You know, Laura's Mac.'

'Oh, yeah,' said Siobhán, 'she wants to have his babies, even though his dad killed her mum, right?'

'I know. I don't think it's fair to her memory. You'd think her daughter would, like, care about stuff like that.'

'But she doesn't, does she?'

'Nope.'

Karen looked me over really coldly from top to toe and was all, 'Sorry, I thought you deserved to know.' But there was a smile on her face that belied that statement utterly. She only said it in case anyone overheard our conversation and realised that I had been right all along and mine were not the ravings of some feral heretic and that Karen actually was the Devil – Satan herself, with soulless eyes that were perfectly defined and empty of all but evil.

I looked around and around and around me but I had nowhere to go; literally EVERYONE was peeing or queuing or preening or eavesdropping and all the stalls were full so I couldn't slam myself into one and hide and I could feel myself just emptying out, like I was falling down a hole or had been spinning and spinning and spinning and finally stopped and the world was still going around and around and I wasn't sure what the world was up to with its dips and wobbles but it was almost certainly malevolent.

Then Felix rang and called me a bitch for not answering my phone before. So there was that.

If life were a film, it would have cut to me falling onto my lonely bed in a world of motherless despair, but life is not a film and I don't have a teleporter, so I went back downstairs and saw everyone still dancing and laughing and doing normal things. But it was like all the fun I had been having had been a dream, and now I had not exactly woken up but more realised that I was dreaming; none of it was real.

The real world is a place that isn't safe, a place you must be careful in, for people are such vulnerable creatures, all soft skin and fragile bones. I've stopped taking supplements since Mum died – she used to have me on calcium and iron and vitamin C and omega 3 and whatever else she liked the sound of in the health-food shop where Sorrel sometimes worked.

Dad doesn't believe in that sort of thing. He says that they are all placebos and the only reason they work is that we are stupid enough to believe in them. This is kind of how Mum felt about God, who Dad actually does believe in. I'm not sure what I think about vitamin tablets. They come in pretty bottles, but what I liked best about them in retrospect was that they showed Mum cared about my health. She considered what I needed and tried her best to make me as strong as I could be. I don't have anyone worrying about ways of boosting my immune system during those cold winter months any more. I have to be as strong as I can be all by myself.

Also, I am no one's favourite person any more. Joel has his family and Ciara has Syzmon, Ella has Mr Cat (and maybe, a bit, Caleb?), Dad has Hedda. (He would deny that Hedda is his favourite person, but she is. He tries to get me out of the way so they can have as much alone time as possible – this is not what one does to one's favourites.)

I forget about how changed the world is now sometimes when I am living life and amn't thinking. But the world is very different and there was no way in hell that I was going to dance in the same circle as the boy whose father killed my mum. Couldn't do it. Couldn't explain to anyone either why I couldn't do it.

I was really worried I would start to cry and I didn't want to cry because I don't want people to think that I'm sad all the time or to always associate me in their heads with death and tears and sorrow. I want to be able to have fun, and I am, but just not constantly. Or not without feeling slightly ashamed afterwards.

Mum would have loved to hear about tonight. Ciara could have come over to our little house and Mum would have helped do our make-up. She wasn't very good at make-up, but she enjoyed the ritual of putting it on before a night out, especially blusher, because she liked the feel of the brush against her cheek. She would have stayed up late to pick us up and make us tea and listen to all the gossip, what people wore and who said what and who kissed who and everything. Sometimes, after she came home from a night out, she'd wake me up and we'd have biscuits and chat. She actually liked talking to me. She listened to my opinions and so on. This is a rare and wonderful quality in a parent. Mum was a rare and wonderful woman.

I decided to get the Nitelink bus home because it was late and I didn't want to have to make awkward conversation with a taxi driver. Also, I felt like walking. The kind of walking that's like swimming, where you go at a rhythmic pace as fast as your two little legs can carry you until the cold wind makes your ears hurt and your mind goes slowly blank as worries ooze out into the air. Suddenly, someone grabbed my elbow. Hard.

As I yanked it away, squaring my shoulders and pulling my arms close to my body, I realised that it was actually Felix. Which was lucky for him, because my next move would have been to scream, 'Fire!' and kick him somewhere vulnerable.

Two options were open to me at this point. I could either burst into a river of snotty tear-gasps or get irate. The latter seemed the safer of the two. Also, I don't appreciate profanity. I have never acted anything but nice to him and also it is SO not my job to mind Ella. So I told him so, brushed him off and kept on walking and was really snippy and monosyllabic when he followed me and tried to make conversation.

He was on his way to find Ella, whom he was supposed to be minding. Mary was gone to Carlow for the weekend and he really didn't want to disturb her. Ella wasn't replying to his texts, which is probably the best course of action if you do not want your night cut short by an overprotective older sibling. Anyway, Felix said he was sorry for calling me a bitch and I said that I accepted his apology. I did not say that it was OK, because I don't think it was OK. I think it was rude and uncalled for, as it happens. I understand that he was upset about Ella; I do. But that does not give him the right to insult me.

'I have to go get her,' he said, meaning Ella, of course.

He was pretty worried about her, and now that he had ascertained that I wasn't going to hold a grudge over the bitch thing he wanted to go to the club and get Ella and take her home by any means necessary.

'You can't do that. She's with a boy.'

It was out before I even thought that maybe I would want to censor it – I mean, it's not any of his business really. Also, it made him even more worried, especially when he heard it was Caleb. I may have ranted a little about Caleb, back around that time he spat at me. I tried explaining that if he followed through with his stupid plan, he would completely humiliate Ella.

'No, I won't. She won't care,' was his incredibly naive response.

I laid out the facts: she is a teenage girl. At her first disco dancey-type affair. With a boy she may or may not be interested in. Then I simply repeated his plans: to go into the club, collect his sister and, in front of everyone, tell her she has to go home because she is not supposed to be out this late.

He nodded and said, 'I see what you mean.'

'Why didn't you just text her and tell her that there was something wrong with Mr Cat? She would have been home in a flash.'

Felix looked at me with respect in his eyes.

'That is EXACTLY what I am going to do. Want to share a taxi home?' (Their house is on the way to my house.)

At this point, I remembered that my house keys were in my overnight bag at Ciara's. I didn't feel like going back but what else was I going to do? It isn't like Mac is a murderer or anything. Just related to a manslaughterer. (Is manslaughterer even a word?)

I wanted Joel. He has an amazing ability to make things seem a little bit better, even when they really, really aren't. I rang him and asked if he wanted to go for chips. But he had gone home already because I had gone and then Kevin had gone and then everyone was kissing everyone else and it was a whole big thing that he wanted no part of. I explained that I had run into Karen in the bathrooms and that she had said something (at this point I teared up) really mean. He was sympathetic but could not come back into town to get me, seeing as how we do not yet have cars of our own or money for endless taxis.

Speaking of money for endless taxis, Joel suggested I ring the moustachioed one, who would no doubt be delighted by my snivelling interruption of his hot date. Only the way he put it was, 'Why don't you ring your dad?'

That made a kind of sense, so I rang Dad and organised that he would pick me up at Ella's house in forty-five minutes or so. He was at Hedda's and had to organise a taxi of his own, seeing as how they like to sip red wine and gaze into each other's eyes as their teeth become stained and their speech becomes emphatic.

Felix and I ran to the taxi rank. We had to run, because if Ella got home before we did and saw that Mr Cat was perfectly all right, her rage would be great.

'How do we make a cat look sick?' asked Felix, poor innocent fellow that he is.

I told him it was pretty much the same as a human: smear some goo around its mouth, press it to a hot water bottle and dampen its brow a little. Also, Mr Cat has a terrible fear of carrots, so if we brandished a carrot or two at him he would probably act all cringey and not himself.

We got home with time – but not much time – to spare. Mr Cat was in his basket, being asleep. He was not best pleased when we woke him up. One look at his grumpy, arrogant little features and I was feeling a little guilty.

'I don't think I can go through with this, Felix.'

'Me neither. He's just too whiskery and aristocratic.'

'Meow,' said Mr Cat, complaining mildly.

'Maybe if we wrap him in a blanket and feed him delicacies that would be a better plan.'

'Yes, let's wrap him in a blanket and feed him delicacies. She will think we are taking care of him.'

And therein lies the power of the cat. No matter what you intend to do, somehow or other it always ends up with delicacies and ear-scratching.

## MR CAT'S FAVOURITE DELICACIES, IN ORDER OF INCREASING YUMMINESS:

### 1

Beef, salmon, chicken. But, weirdly, not ham. Mr Cat hates ham almost as much as he is frightened of carrots. He hisses when he smells a slice.

## 2

Catnip. Ella grows her own in a pot in her room. Mr Cat loves that pot. He will sometimes rub himself against it for what to him probably seems like minutes, but to us is actually, like, an hour and a half to three hours. Mr Cat has a problem.

## 3

Cream. Mr Cat loves cream. He gets disappointed when given a saucer of milk because it is not cream. He will stare at it endlessly, wondering why it is not cream, give it one cursory lick in case he was wrong and it was cream all along, and then stalk off disappointedly, possibly to Ella's room to nip his sorrows in the bud with a visit to his special pot of drugs.

## 4

Cheese. Mr Cat enjoys a variety of fine cheeses. Especially when cut into chunks. If you hold a chunk of cheese in the air, he will go on his hind legs and do a little 'give me cheese' dance of shame. It is the least dignified activity he engages in and this shows how much he values cheese. 'He will not do a dance for meat/ he will not wobble on his feet/ but if you take a cube of cheese/ then he will do the dance of please' is a song Felix, Ella and I have made up especially for the cheese dance.

5

Cream cheese on a cat treat you get in a shop. Mr Cat likes cream. Mr Cat likes cheese. The marriage of the two entrances him on a whole new level. If someone ever comes up with a way to put cream cheese into cubes, I think he would die from an excess of wonderment.

When Ella got home, I was dozing on the sofa beside Felix, who was also dozing on the sofa. Mr Cat was on the kitchen counter, quickly working his way through an entire block of cheddar that he was only supposed to be given a bit of.

(I forgot to mention 6

Anything that is on a counter.)

Ella put the cheese away, conducted a full physical examination on Mr Cat, woke us up and told us that the rest of the night had been fun, that Dolphin Laura and Mac had left early to go to a house party of some description, and that Ciara was sad because she thought I was mad at her. (I texted her on the way home to say

Not mad at you. Sorry for leaving early. Long story involving Karen and drama. Didn't punch her, though. Will chat soon xoxo p.s. make me a hat.

Hopefully that'll do the job.)

Also, Caleb held Ella's hand on the way to the taxi rank. They walked there with Ciara and Syzmon.

I was all, 'That's exciting!' because even if I disapprove of Caleb, I approve of Ella being happy.

Felix was all, 'I don't like this Caleb fellow.' I told him to stop sounding like a forty-year-old. At this point in time, the phone rang. It was Dad. He was in a taxi, and so I hugged them both goodbye (Ella doesn't really like hugs but I wanted to hug Felix so I pretended like I was a huggy person in order to get what I wanted. MUHAHAHAHA) and headed off.

Fintan, Lord of the Realm, Member of the Golf Club, Grower of the Moustache Joel Once Considered Cool, Owner of the Huge House in Which I Live, was not best pleased that his date had been cut short. He had been trying to convince Hedda not to have doubts about moving in together or something. I didn't care, I just wanted to be at home, home where nobody ever uses the word 'smoosh' in an inappropriate manner.

'How was the disco?' asked Fintan. (When he was young, club/dancey events were called discos and shoulder pads were the new hotness.)

'OK,' I said, aware that the taxi driver was listening.

Anyway, we got home, stopping (oh, my!) for chips on the way. We finished them at the kitchen table.

'Why didn't you stay at Ciara's?' Dad asked.

'Urrrgh. Long story.'

'Did you two have a row?'

'No. It was Karen. She said some things.'

'About your ridiculous ballerina skirt?'

Dad hates my tutu. Because he knows nothing about what is or isn't pretty.

'NO! My skirt is awesome. About Mum.'

'Oh. That's much worse.'

'Mmmm.'

And so, in an uncharacteristically open and honest move, I told Dad what Karen had said, leaving out the part about me fancying Mac and feeling like a big dirty betrayer for my lustful thoughts.

He was appropriately irate with her and called her 'a little wagon'. Also, he suggested that she was jealous of my 'intelligence and beauty', which is such a sweetly deluded dad-ish thing to say that I burst out laughing and promptly felt a little better.

He also wanted to go into school and tell Ms Cleary about Karen being the Devil, but I told him not to bother. It would just give her more of a reason to hate me. Sigh.

Anyway, after about an hour of chatting about Brian McAllister and how it's not his family's fault he did such a dreadful thing but how they should still stay the hell away from us, because being reminded of the circumstances of Mum's death sucks as hard as a barnacle on a ship's hull, we toddled off to bed.

But I couldn't switch my brain off so I scribbled and ranted a bit at poor sleepy Roderick, who is hiding under his fleecy blanket in a manful attempt to drown out the music I have on in the background. It's about four in the morning now, so he is right to want to get some rest. I might have to emulate the little furry grumpus, or else my hot water bottle will get cold and I'll have to make a new one all over again. And that would NEVER do.

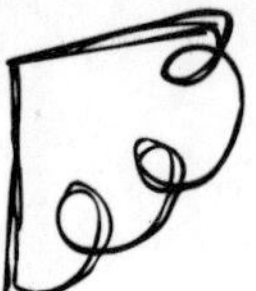

**ACCOUTREMENTS:** Bits 'n' bobs, paraphernalia, stuff that goes along with other stuff. Accoutrements are usually related to a specific thing. For example, accoutrements that go with Ciara's GHD include a misting bottle full of water and a special serum for hair smoothening. Accoutrements that go with her sewing machine include bobbins of thread, needles, pins, a foot pedal, a box full of cloth and a special scissors that came with its own sharpener.

**ASSIDUOUS:** Caring, mindful. I would like a boyfriend who was assiduous about being nice to me. But I would not like a boyfriend who was assiduous about pointing out my physical imperfections. Sometimes I worry that when I finally do get kissed, whoever kisses me will swoop in and then notice the blackheads on my nose and be all 'eww' and run away. Ciara does not share this fear because she has Syzmon and no imperfections.

***GRANDES DAMES* OF THE THEATRE:** A *grande dame* of the theatre is a fancy old actress who is very important and wears fur coats and jewels she got from admirers in her gilded youth. In my head, a *grande dame* of the theatre has a British accent, but I suppose a Russian or French one would also be acceptable.

**PLATEAUING:** Levelling out. A plateau is a flat surface up high, so if something goes flat for a while, while being up high it is plateauing.

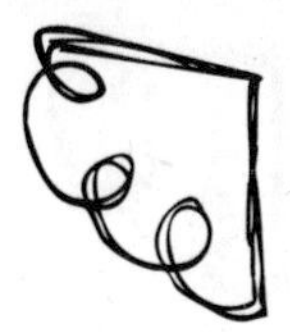

**ADJACENCE:** The state of being near to, just around the corner from. My adjacence to Felix often causes me to break out in tingles and fantasies in which I am the lead character in a romantic comedy where he will do anything to win my heart. It's pretty pathetic how needy fantasy-Felix can be. He is lucky fantasy-me puts up with him.

**LENIENT:** Lax, permissive. Parents who say things like, 'I'd rather you drink/smoke/take speed at home than out on the streets like a delinquent,' are permissive. Also parents who let their kids get LOADS of piercings and tattoos. But the second way to be permissive is better than the first because piercings and tattoos are lovely. If I were allowed to, I would get my lip pierced and also get a tattoo of a cowslip on my ribcage, just under my heart, in memory of my mum. People called her 'Bláth', which means flower, and cowslips were her favourite bloom of all.

**PROMISCUOUS:** Sexually free-spirited. Getting a lot of play. Sometimes the word 'slutty' is used to describe promiscuous women but only by haters. I think that people should be allowed to get with each other as much or as little as they like, unless they are hurting someone or endangering their health. **WARNING: Excessive promiscuity can lead to HIV or putting your back out.**

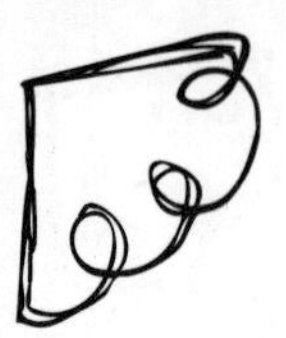
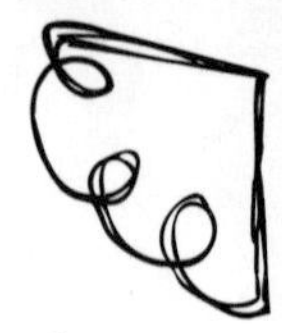

**INCLEMENT:** Not clement. Wet, cold, rotten Irish weather is inclement. Which is weird, because I have NEVER heard someone exclaim, 'Ooh, look how clement the weather is today! Not a cloud in the sky. Yay for clemency in terms of weather!!!'

**CONTRABAND:** Things you are not supposed to have, for example alcohol, drugs and firearms. I think that half the fun of drinking when you are too young to do it legally is the fact that it is contraband and therefore terribly bold behaviour altogether.

**VOYEURISM:** The 'ism' of the word voyeur. Voyeur is basically a tarted-up way of saying peeping Tom. If you get off on looking at up-skirt videos on YouTube, you are a voyeur. If you have a peephole that goes into a changing room and you look through it like a dirty pervert, then you are a voyeur. If you walk into a room and two people are hooking up and don't notice you and instead of walking away like a normal human being you take a seat and stare at them with watery bulge-eyes, then you are a voyeur. Who engages in voyeurism.

**EMPHATIC:** A potent mixture of definite and enthusiastic. The way people talk when they are trying to convince you of their deeply held beliefs or telling you that you are not allowed to get a facial piercing.

# A NAME: SOMETHING FISH HAVE, SOMETHING SUNNED-ON SKIN DOES (6)

Dad is letting me transfer to another swimming club because I don't really want to be around Laura the Human Dolphin.

I wonder if she knew who I was. If she did, I think it was a bit insensitive of her to be all friendly and stuff. I mean, she is going out with the boy whose dad killed my mum and that is a decidedly side-taking move.

I can't believe I didn't cop about Mac earlier. I mean, the clues were there, even if they were more cryptic than simplex. The dad-not-being-able-to-drive thing was a big clue. Also the Mac bit of his name.

I can't believe Brian McAllister has such a handsome son. It surely is nature's way of compensating for being the offspring of a drunken killer. He'd probably rather be ugly and have a dad who didn't go to prison, though.

Although I doubt Laura the Human Dolphin would go out with a boy who wasn't good-looking. Not that she's shallow, it's sort of that she's so pretty herself that it would just look wrong.

Karen was very smug at school on Monday. But then Caleb, in a fit of kindly disloyalty, told me that she waxes her neck. Her hairline starts at the top of her back, you see, so if she didn't wax it regularly she would resemble some sort of human/chimp hybrid. I know that this is nothing to be ashamed of and has nothing to do with her being the Devil, but it did make me feel a bit better.

I told them about Mac on Monday. I kind of needed the weekend to mull it over and decide how I felt about it. And how I feel is this: I don't hate Mac or Laura, but I don't want to be around them any more than is absolutely necessary, because of the negative associations with a man I think I am perfectly justified in hating.

Also, I hate Karen now. Before I was just aware that she was the Devil, but now I feel that she is the Devil and I am a priest who needs to learn the rites of exorcism in order to stop the Devil ruining further social events.

Also, next time there is a night out, Ciara and I are both going to wear hats. She is making me a rat-themed one. It will probably have a rat on it, but she will neither confirm nor deny this guess.

She is making a lily-themed one for Grandma Lily as well. It is hard to find an artificial lily that does not look dreadful. That is what Syzmon and Ciara have been up to all weekend. Well, that and playing football. Ciara went to Syzmon's match with Leona because Leona's brother is on the team as well. They won and stuff. Apparently it was a really good game, but I know if I had been there I would not have been able to tell until the cheering started. For all my smarts, I always feel a little bit dumb when it comes to sports and sports-related things. I am uncoordinated and while I know that the objective is generally to get the ball in the hole, I find the scoring systems both complex and really, really dull. Ciara doesn't. She knows the offside rule and can explain it in terms an idiot can understand.

# THE OFFSIDE RULE

If you are nearer to the other team's goal than the ball and the second last other team member then you are offside. But do not panic! It is not a crime in itself to be offside. That would be very counterproductive.

If your team has the ball and you are interfering with the play in a way that suits your guys but is not fair on the other guys, then the referee can invoke the offside rule and award a kick to the other team.

Ciara used a little picture to explain this and I am writing it down because I will probably forget it soon and I want to remember that there was a time, a glorious, glorious time, when I knew a bit more about football than the next man. Although this only applies if the next man is Joel's little brother Marcus, and he'll probably catch up to me sooner rather than later. Joel's dad loves sport, so Joel knows a lot about it by default.

Joel knows a lot about lots of things. That is why people warm to him and tell him their shameful secrets. He came over Saturday evening after the meeting with Kevin. There were pros and also cons to this meeting. They went to a place that had amazing hazelnut brownies, which was a pro. They laughed and chatted and made merry – also a pro. Kevin got all serious after a while and looked Joel in the eyes and said, 'I haven't been completely honest with you.' For a second Joel contemplated taking Kevin's hand, but being the reticent fellow that he is, decided against it.

Then Kevin went on to explain that he had a secret (yes!) and that he was worried people might judge him (yes!) but he felt comfortable around Joel (yes!) and thought he might be the kind of person who would understand why he does the things he does (yes ...?)

Joel nodded and tried to look sexily understanding.

And then Kevin told him that he LARPs.

**RETICENT:** Shy, not offering loads of personal information readily. Joel is only reticent about being gay. Normally he is very good at not being shy. I am very bad at not being shy and normally get very reticent and mumbly when confronted with a group of new people. Sometimes I am even reticent about telling stuff to not-new people, which is why Ciara only found out that Brian McAllister was out of prison when I was telling her about the Mac thing. I could tell from her face that she was annoyed not to have been told but she didn't give out to me because I had been through enough after my confrontation with the Devil.

## HE IS A LARPER.
## A LARPER.
## OH GOOD GOD.

LARP stands for *live action role-play*. It involves elaborate costumes and battles and playing pretend and swords and wands and worlds in which there is the possibility of dragons and so on and so forth.

The best thing is that when Kevin told Joel this, he was all, 'That's grand. And by the way, I'm gay.' Because his secret was cooler than Kevin's one. I was really pleased by this admission. He is one step closer to telling either Ciara or his parents.

Also, next Saturday afternoon, the two of us are going LARPing with Kevin, just to show him that we understand and that there is nothing to be ashamed of. It is what it is; he's not doing any harm to anyone. So there's that.

I'm not exactly sure how to feel. I knew LARPers existed but I never thought I'd actually have one in my social circle. Live and let live, I suppose. I'd be lying if I said it didn't sort of disgust me. It just isn't natural. All those wizards with their invisible lightning bolts that nobody can see but everyone pretends are there. I mean, if God had intended for us to shoot imaginary lightning bolts out of our hands after performing some sort of dramatic sweeping gesture, surely that's what we'd all be doing, right?

Anyway, it doesn't matter what I think because I'm mostly going to support Joel, who is mostly going to support Kevin, in a fit of some sort of weird karmic reasoning which means that he thinks that his dad will be OK with him liking boys if he is OK with the boy he likes liking this ridiculously nerdy thing. I get it. Sort of.

I am trying to convince myself that it will be fun, in a sort of ironic, Hallowe'en-every-day-of-the-year way. Also, I get to wield a staff. Which is fodder for much hilarity – especially if it's magic. Because then you can say, 'I'll just get my staff to do it' and it's as though you have servants, only you don't; you just have a big wooden stick that does pretend magic.

Joel is worried that he will never get a boyfriend, at least not until he goes to college. I have this worry too but he dismissed it because the laws of probability give me a bigger chance of boy action than they give Joel. Also, he wants to have a lovely boyfriend his own age or maybe six to eighteen months older, as opposed to some middle-aged man on the Internet.

To which I responded, 'Have you been looking for love in all the wrong places, Joel?' He would not give me a straight answer. I thoroughly approve of the net nanny system his parents have in place. They are sensible, pervert-thwarting heroes.

I would like to find Joel a boy who loves him. But first I want a boy who loves me. I'm selfish that way. It must be nice to have someone to hold your hand and kiss you and think you're wonderful even when you have sticky-uppy hair like a giraffe. I need to get my hair touched up again. And that's not all I need to get touched up. Oh, my.

This is the level of discourse that Joel and I descended to on Saturday. It was hilarious at the time but, looking back, it was kind of terrifying and exactly the reason I would never go on a reality TV show. Because what is absolutely funny and wonderful on one day could, if played back to you and re-edited to make sure everyone got the full effect of your braying donkey laugh, kind of break your tiny little heart. Or my tiny little heart anyway. And that's been broken enough for one lifetime.

I have to go and drink tea with Grandma Lily and Ciara tomorrow night. Well, myself and Ciara will be drinking tea. Lily will be drinking gin out of teacups. She has started having a gin or two as a nightcap in order to be able to turn down Ciara's parents when they ask her to drop them places.

'She's not supposed to be driving, Primrose,' Ciara said on the phone. Her voice sounded like her forehead was all wrinkled with worry. 'That's half the reason that they convinced her to come and live with us – so they could look after her, seeing as she's not really able to look after herself any more. And it's not like she takes that much looking after. I mean, I make her supper every night and dinner two nights a week. And Lord knows I have enough on my plate without worrying about the two of them.'

Ciara actually does have a lot on her plate. Her mum is always making her do things around the house and buying her elaborate skincare products for the acne problem that she does not have. Ciara cleanses, tones and moisturises her eyes and the rest of her face separately. This necessitates six different products and a fine linen facecloth.

I just whack a facecloth on and scrub till my eyes have thick grey circles around them, whereupon I lash a handful of moisturiser (sometimes hand cream) on, but only if I feel like it. Now, some might say that this is probably why I have breakouts and Ciara does not, but some would be completely off base there. It is genetics. That is what it is. Mum was still getting breakouts when she died and she was in her thirties. I have never seen Ciara's mum with so much as a blackhead. She hardly even has pores. Maybe she is a vampire.

## FINTAN

Fintan has a fin-plan. I came across Hedda's contraceptive pills in the cutlery drawer yesterday morning. I gave them to Dad with a suitably disgusted expression on my face (I mean, who does that?) and told him to ring her and give them back.

Then on Wednesday I found them slotted into the middle of a packet of those cereal bars he likes that I find disgusting. (I was out of lunch things.)

**CONTRACEPTIVE PILLS:** Pills you take if you want to have sex but do not want babies. Hedda should definitely be taking them. For the moment.

This is not a good sign. Hedda is supposed to be moving in this Friday but she is totally going to put it off because she has planned a weekend away with friends. They are going to visit another friend who lives in Venice and is a glass-blower. (Hedda is way cooler than Fintan. I have no idea why they are together.)

I began to suspect that something was amiss because of the cereal-bar incident and also because when I said, 'You don't want a new baby, do you?' (by way of explaining why he should return his girlfriend's medication which she needs to take daily), he was all muttery and, 'Well, that wouldn't be the worst thing in the world, now, would it?'

I confirmed that it would, in fact, be one of the worst things in the world, if not the very worst.

I could tell from the guilty look on his face that there was something he was trying to hide. It only took a few minutes of thorough questioning to weasel it out of him.

'Dad?'

'Yes, Prim.'

'Have you been, like, plotting to get Hedda pregnant?'

'No. NO. No. Er ... why do you ask?'

(I knew from his triple no that the answer to my question was yes. Denying something too much is almost the same as not denying it at all.)

Then came the bit where I got a bit hypothetical to rein him in.

'So, say if Hedda was planning to break up with you, do you reckon she'd stay if you guys were going to have a baby?'

'She probably would, yes.'

'Oh my God, Fintan! You have been scheming for babies. You are a baby-schemer. Have you no respect for a woman's reproductive rights?'

'I have not. Anyway, "scheming for babies" isn't even a thing. There's no such thing as "scheming for babies".'

Sadly, scheming for babies is EXACTLY what Fintan, Lord Lieutenant of Intelligent Living, had been doing. I know this because the next part of our conversation involved the phrase 'don't tell Hedda'.

'So, Fintan.'

'Yes, Primrose.'

'Let me tell you why the hypothetical baby-scheming you're doing would be a terrible idea. Apart from the fact that it is morally repugnant on several levels.'

'Go on.'

**REPRODUCTIVE RIGHTS:** The right to not be forced to have babies you don't want. I am slightly confused about this, I will admit, because I was an accidental baby that my mum wasn't ready for. So I am glad that she decided to keep me. But on the other hand, one should not be forced to have Fintan's babies simply because he has purloined one's contraceptives in a fit of needy.

**PURLOINING:** Well, it doesn't have a thing to do with loins, I'll tell you that right now. Get your mind out of the gutter. The idea! It means stealing but sounds kind of fancy. I would rather be arrested for establishment-purloining than shoplifting. It has a certain class about it. Roderick is forever purloining things to nibble and inspect. He is the greatest thief the world has ever known. Also the cutest.

'It is needy. And needy is the death-knell for any relationship. Once one person starts being all needy, the other person becomes callous and uncaring in order to balance things out.'

'That doesn't happen.'

So I reminded him of Cynthia and Margaret and Mum's ex, Andrew, who texted twenty times a day even though he was a grown-up man.

The tale of Andrew in particular seemed to sober Dad right up. Not that he was drunk. Except on his own vulnerability.

It is a strange and creepy world, the world of the middle-aged businessman. Personally I reckon he should chill the hell out. I mean, if Hedda wants to be with him, that's great, but if she doesn't that's fine too. It's not like she does all that much for him or that they spend that much time together even. They just go on dates a few times a week.

I don't know. I can't deal with all this, really. I'd just go mad. Because it isn't funny; its kind of unhinged and worrying that Dad would go so mental trying to hang on to a woman that might not even love him back, and yet he regularly forgets that I need lifts and money and dinners and things. Not all the time; not even most of the time. But still, regularly enough for it to be noticed. Written down in my little mental book of things he has done, to be taken out and alluded to whenever we have a row. He thinks that's petty but I kind of feel justified in being petty. I'm a teenage girl; we're supposed to be all unreasonable and cranky and full of hormones that lead to mood swings and burgeoning boobage. And, as Mum used to tell me her mother used to say, 'It wasn't from the ground I licked it.'

Fintan is petty as a miniature Chihuahua. Sometimes, after I have been late out of school or town or wherever, he will make a point of being exactly that late to the minute the next time he has to come and get me.

He calls that teaching me a lesson. I agree. The lesson is that he is at least twice as petty as I am, so accusations of pettiness that come out of his stupid furry mouth are moot.

I told Lily and Ciara about it while we were watching Rock Hudson come on to Doris Day. They think it is basically criminal. (Not RH coming on to DD; the Dad thing.)

'I had a pregnancy every year from ages nineteen to thirty-four,' said Grandma Lily. 'I love my children but they were a great deal of work. I wouldn't wish an unwanted baby on my worst enemy.'

'So how many kids do you have?'

'Four, Prim. I had fifteen pregnancies, but only five babies. The rest of them all died. Except for Ciara's aunt Cecilia, who lived for three weeks before she left us.'

What do you say to that? I don't know but what I did say is, 'That must have been hard.'

'Well, I'd be lying if I said it didn't take its toll on my body. I was quite flat-chested when I got married, Primrose. About the same size as Ciara, here.'

She sipped her gin resentfully while we took a moment to assess her massive rack.

'I am never having kids,' said Ciara, who is an A-cup and proud of it.

Grandma Lily considered her favourite grandchild fondly.

'Well, not until you're good and ready, at any rate. Good and ready. And married.'

This last bit was followed with a surprisingly steely glare.

I chose not to bring up my own dodgily unmarried parental situation. I mean, she probably knows. And it's not like the out-of-wedlock baby-having worked out oh-so-splendidly for them.

I wonder what sort of a father Brian McAllister is. Not a very good one for the past two years, probably, seeing as how you can't be a very good father when you are in prison, by virtue of being almost completely absent from the lives of your children.

He isn't a handsome man. It's weird that his son is such a fox. Maybe he has a really pretty wife who is having an affair with a neighbour so obsessed with her that he is going to murder BMcA and make it look like a terrible accident. I think about stuff like that sometimes and then I feel guilty. Because an eye for an eye is all well and good, but who's to say what value an eye has?

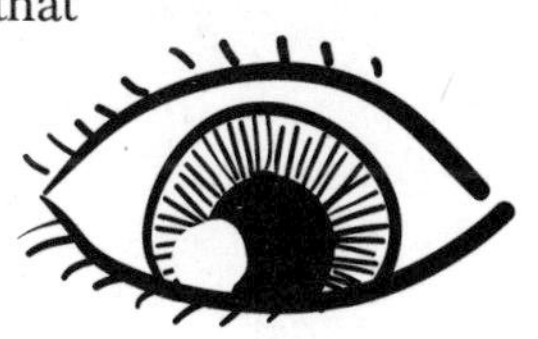

If it was to be really fair, I should be allowed to go back in time and kill his mother now, but I don't think I'd want to. This whole Mac-being-a-McAllister thing is really messing with my head; it is looping and sweeping like it used to do in the months just after Mum died. It isn't good. I should probably have said something about it to Ciara but she didn't like how I liked Mac in the first place, and ... I don't know. It just feels like something I should keep safely squished inside until it dies.

I mean, it's not like I even knew him properly. It's sort of like finding out Alfric, the sexy Viking from my favourite sexy Viking book, was related to Brian McAllister. It shouldn't matter. But it's like, if random crushes are tainted by the guy who killed my mum, will I ever be able to get away from it? I mean, I don't want to forget her or anything. Of course not that, but I don't want my life to be defined by tragedy either. I don't want to be always being reminded to be sad.

**LUSTROUS:** Shiny, sheeny, sparkly and reflective. It is a good quality in hair but a bad quality in bald heads. Not that they should be dirty or matte, but those ones that look particularly polished creep me out.

**TAINTED:** Made dirty or poisoned somehow. Like, I really like Doris Day but then I read online when I got home that she wasn't very nice about gay people and that kind of tainted her for me. Because now I associate her with being a toolbox full of bigotry.

## THE FIRST ONE IS NOT THE SHALLOWEST (3)

Dad is making me so mad today. I was innocently making myself a cup of coffee by way of breakfast when he came in and got all starey and noticey about the cuts on my legs. I thought he had already left, and they were pretty itchy, which is why I had my pyjama short-shorts on as opposed to some sort of capri pants, which would have made matters a little easier.

I tried to explain to him that I had just been extra clumsy while shaving my legs but he was all on his high horse and ranting about self-harm and cries for help and other things he has read about on the Internet.

'I am not going to lose you, Primrose,' he declared dramatically, and gave me a withering look when I pointed out that since we were both in the kitchen, even should he lose me I would probably be incredibly easy to find.

'Start at the larder, because that's where the biscuits are kept,' I offered helpfully.

'That's not what I meant,' he growled. 'Stop distracting me from your problems.'

I think I am going to be sent back to counselling. Which kind of sucks because I was pretty happy being normal and well-adjusted, apart from the odd bump. Fintan is a very silly man who is playing fast and loose with his money.

Things got a bit yelly after that, especially when I told him that I couldn't go for a one-on-one session this weekend because I was going LARPing with Joel.

He was all, 'No you're not!' and then, 'What's LARPing when it's at home?' Then when I explained he decided he needed to move the appointment up anyway because, 'This is worse than I thought.'

That may have been a joke – he tried to make conversation about swords over dinner, which he actually cooked. I was having none of it, though. I am not talking to him. He is a large-nosed meddler who is always trying

to control me. I will not be controlled. I am a wildflower, for goodness' sake. None can prune me! Nor should they.

He can go hang. That is a Grandma Lily saying, passed along through Ciara. Also 'There is more than one way to skin a cat.'

Welcome to the family, Hedda! Every day a new adventure. God. If I were Hedda, I'd want to stay the hell away from the both of us as well.

I wonder does Dad meddle in her life? Also, who she will side with in the inevitable rows she will soon become a party to? I hope me, out of a sort of feminist solidarity. But I can't be sure because she does like Dad as well, even if he is a creep who has considered trying to get her pregnant without her knowledge. He is the one who needs therapy, not me. All I do is get oddly clumsy and sometimes cry myself to sleep out of a sensible and rational despair because Mum isn't around any more.

And also sometimes because everyone hates me and no one understands me and I feel fat and my favourite pair of shoes are scuffed in a way that means I can't really get away with wearing them any more.

Mum would understand all these woes. Dad doesn't. I mean, if I get him on his own he'll listen and make clucking noises that are supposed to convey understanding, like some sort of badly assembled robot that has no idea what human beings are actually like. But even when Mum didn't understand, she spent more time trying to than Dad does, asking the right questions and rubbing the back of my head as if I were a soft little she-rat who needed a calming massage at the end of a long day.

Isn't it weird that when I rub Roderick it comforts both of us? You'd think one of us would get more out of it than the other, but no. Look at him now, his little face all burrowed in the crook of my elbow, snuggling furiously as if his life depended on it. And who knows? Maybe it does a bit.

I once read about an experiment this guy did on little baby monkeys, where he gave them a soft cuddly mum and a wire mother who had sharp edges. The wire mother had the food, but the little baby monkeys starved themselves rather than sacrifice their snuggles.

I'm off again. Weep, weep, weep. It's just ... their little faces all wizened and brave-looking, like little brown-eyed hairy grannies. Roderick would have found a way to steal the food from the wire mother, I reckon. And then he and the cuddly mother would have broken out of that hellhole, never to be heard from again. Rats are highly intelligent creatures. Intelligent, acrobatic and whiskery. Fine qualities all.

But weirdly, I'm really looking forward to LARPing now. There's something about parental disapproval that makes things more exciting.

Maybe I should get Ciara to ask Grandma Lily for advice about the whole Dad-getting-all-up-in-my-face thing. Only without mentioning his cutting theory because that is exactly the kind of thing that Ciara would overreact about, and I don't need any more drama. At all. Ever. Unless it is boy drama, in which case, bring it on, world.

## CUT

Grandma Lily had a stroke last night. Ciara wasn't at school today. It's kind of scary and horrible, even though she's old and everyone was kind of expecting her to die.

I hate sick people, dying people, reminding me how mortal we all are. I know it's not their fault. Another thing I hate is funerals. It seems so forced, like we all have to be sad at this one place for this period of time and then we get over ourselves and get back to living.

Grief – real grief – doesn't work like that. It can't – it won't – be fettered. I hate funerals. Everyone wearing black and being sorry. No one is really sorry, though. No one wishes it had happened to them instead of you.

She isn't even dead yet, Grandma Lily, but Joel was acting as if it was only a matter of time, because his uncle Thomas had a stroke and died soon after and he was a lot younger and stronger than Lily. I kind of snapped at him about it because he was acting like it was no big deal, even though he's met Lily and everything. He was way more interested in what we were going to wear to go LARPing and what the story was with my dad and Hedda.

Joel is fascinated by the fact that my dad has a love life. It is probably because his parents have always been together his whole life. He kind of sees girlfriends/boyfriends as things that teenagers are supposed to have but old people aren't really. Also, he's very into relationship problems because they make him feel better about not having a boyfriend.

I am too. I mean, I'd be quite entertained if Syzmon and Ciara were to have some sort of dramatic bust-up involving cheating and a dashing new exchange student from Nordic climes (secret sexy Viking!). It would give me an opportunity to say things that people say in movies and magazine articles, like 'The heart wants what it wants' and 'He's not worth it; you're way better off without him. I can't believe he stole the chalices from your local monastery and burned it to the ground.'

But when it's your parents, it's kind of different. Not necessarily with Mum, although sometimes I could get a bit cringey when she wanted to do boyfriend talk – not so much when I was at the embarrassing 'boys are disgusting, except for Joel and sometimes even including Joel' stage, but when I got to the even more embarrassing 'boys are disgusting except for sometimes when I inexplicably get the urge to smell their hair' stage. I'm still stuck on that, actually, but with a definite view to graduating to kissing and/or fondling sometime soon.

FONDLING is a FILTHY word, actually. If you break it up it sounds OK – something you might do to someone that you are fond of. But if I ever turned to Felix with a gleam in my eye and said, 'Felix, baby (I call him baby because this daydream takes place in a dive bar somewhere in America), I want to FONDLE you,' he would probably block me on Facebook and then move house.

Joel thinks Fintan is mad to want to have another baby with Hedda.

'The only reason people have children is so they can boast about them to other people and eventually be taken care of when they get disgustingly old and need to wear adult nappies with names that try to sound dignified like "Absorbtimate". If I had a line of them, I'd call them "Old Soaks" and make them in 1940s floral patterns.'

'Ew. Anyway, that is not the only reason people have kids, Joel.'

'It totally is. And you're clever and will probably be nice to him when he's old so you can inherit all his money.'

'I'd be nice to him anyway. Probably. So, if that's all kids are for, what's the point of Marcus?'

'I am the heir and Marcus is the spare, in case I go off and live in Panama or somewhere.'

'Hmmm. Maybe another baby wouldn't be the worst thing in the world. Also it would distract the two of them a lot and I could get up to mischief. I don't get up to half enough mischief.'

'Me neither.'

It is sadly true; I don't get up to half enough mischief. Considering how much Fintan gives out to me, you'd swear I was a bratty teenage drunkard and not an embarassingly sensible girl of the nerdly persuasion.

I don't want Lily to die. She's fun and Ciara loves her and she drinks gin of a Wednesday afternoon and giggles like a little bird when she is amused. Also, she does not wear Old Soaks, so she always smells nice. Kind of flowery.

I don't want Ciara to stop talking like a little old lady and knowing how to play gin rummy and bridge.

When Fintan is old and I do have to take care of him, I wonder will I resent it? Because I have things to do as well. Ciara's mum kind of resents having Lily in the house even though Lily is very careful not to tell her how to run her home because that would lead to friction. Lily is very big on a lack of friction, on keeping things running smoothly, powered by rosaries and flower-arranging classes at the community centre and daily doses of car-avoiding gin. I wonder what effect the stroke will have on the little life she has built here? Ciara says it is too soon to tell what will happen, but she might have to learn how to talk again or walk again or how to brush her teeth and write.

**JAPANESE LOVE MOTEL:** A motel in Japan where you can rent rooms by the hour for the purposes of doing it. I read about them online and they sounded like something Karen would be into. For clone-sex and plotting my downfall.

I can't imagine having to re-learn how to write. It took so bloody long the first time. Especially joined-up writing, which is the work of the Devil and so is probably somehow Karen's fault. Karen wasn't in today because she was meeting Satan in a Japanese love motel for illicit fire-sex.

The most disturbing thing about it is that she and Satan are THE SAME PERSON, so it was basically clone-sex, which is the worst kind of incest. Must remember to tell Joel about clone-sex. He will be thoroughly disgusted.

**PARTNER:** What grown-ups call their boyfriends or girlfriends. Like 'I live with my partner' or 'My Partner and I enjoy couples bowling and laughing at our own jokes'. (I enjoy laughing at my own jokes too, but only when they are funny. And I'm not, like, proud of it or anything.)

Hedda is Dad's partner and he is hers, even though I hardly ever see her any more. When they first got together, I used to see her about once a week. Since Dad proposed, it is kind of like she is avoiding me. Although I think she is also avoiding Dad so I'm not taking it personally. Well, I am a bit, I suppose. But if I had a problem that necessitated a grown-up woman it'd be Sorrel or Méadhbh or Mary or Anne I would ring before I'd even think of bothering Hedda. She is partners with my dad but she is not my step-mother figure at all.

If I am ever someone's partner, I will call them partner all the time like a sexily drawling cowboy. 'Partner,' I will say, 'can you pick up a pint of milk on the way home?' Picking up a pint of milk on the way home is a very partner thing to do. When teenagers are in a couple they hold hands, laugh at each other's jokes and enjoy varying levels of sexy-time. But when you're an adult it's all 'pick up a pint of milk'. If I had a boyfriend, I would not care about milk or lack of milk unless I needed it to quench my thirst after some energetic hug-and-kissing sessions. I'm not super gone on milk anyway. I hardly ever drink it on its own, only in hot drinks or on cereal.

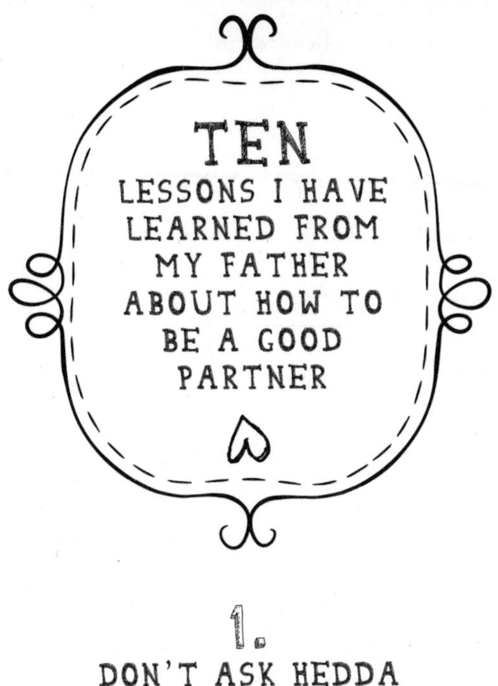


## 1.

## DON'T ASK HEDDA TO MARRY YOU.

Well, not that I was planning to. But what I took from the whole proposal thing is not to ask someone to take a big relationship step unless you're pretty sure they'll say yes. Things like marriage should be mutual decisions, as opposed to needy attempts to sweep the less interested, more desirable party off his or her feet. Like, I would never ask a boy I was kissing if he wanted to be my boyfriend. I would just wait for things to move that way and hope he'd refer to me as his girlfriend at some stage.

Not that it's the boy's job to do all of the running. If I were a boy, or a girl who liked girls, I think I would still be the same. The person who is not me should make more of an effort because then they will be slightly unsure of me and thus fancy me more with each passing day.

## 2.

## DON'T MAKE YOUR GIRLFRIENDS RUN ERRANDS FOR YOU AS THOUGH THEY WERE SOME SORT OF PERSONAL ASSISTANT WITH KISSING DUTIES.

Dad was a divil for doing this, getting Anna or Cynthia or whoever he was seeing at the time to pick up dry-cleaning, change sheets, wash up and pick me up from after-school activities whenever Mum couldn't do it.

Fair play to him for being such a hot commodity that otherwise sensible women are only too happy to be treated like slaves by him. People don't take advantage of people they properly care about. If you're taking advantage of the person you are going out with, you probably don't properly care about them and should break up with them before you accrue a lot of really bad karma and need to get Sorrel to cleanse your chakras, lest the person you eventually really love begin to take advantage of you.

Dad would never let Sorrel at his chakras but sometimes I think he should. I have no idea what chakras are but I think it is to do with bad energy and good energy. Making Cynthia file his tax returns created a LOT of bad energy because it was a mean thing to do. And eventually, if you do a lot of mean things, you become a mean person. And nobody wants to spend huge amounts of time hugging and kissing a mean person.

## 3.
## IF YOU TAKE SOMEONE FOR GRANTED AND BREAK UP WITH THEM BY EMAIL, DO NOT EXPECT TO REMAIN ON GOOD TERMS WITH THEM.

Dad seems genuinely perplexed when women he has been an ass to are irate and bitter about it post-break-up. He says things like, 'She didn't mind about that at the time.'

Only she did. She just didn't say anything because she didn't want you to break up with her in a terse cliché of an email.

## 4.
## IF YOU LIKE SOMEONE ENOUGH YOU WON'T 'NEED SPACE'.

## 5.
## IF SOMEONE PREFERS THE IDEA OF BEING WITH SPACE TO BEING WITH YOU, YOU SHOULD BREAK UP WITH THEM PROMPTLY.

Space is not all that great. Unless you are an astronaut, and even then I imagine there are boring bits once you get used to looking out the window and being amongst the stars.

I don't think there are any Irish astronauts. Maybe I could be the first. Space suits look really comfy, like big mobile sleeping cocoons. If I were an astronaut, I would probably spend most of my time sleeping.

## 6.

## IF SOMEONE IS WORKING LATE, DO NOT STORM INTO THEIR OFFICE ACCUSING THEM OF AFFAIRS.

This has happened to my father twice. I know, because I was hanging out with Sheila (my dad's secretary) when Cynthia stormed in, ready for a big confrontation. Sheila told me it was not the first time. Dad's girlfriends often suspect Fintan of cheating on them with Sheila, but that could never happen because she is thirteen years older than him and way out of his league.

## 7.

## IF SOMEONE WORKS LATE ALL THE TIME, MAYBE THEY ARE WORKING LATE BECAUSE THEY DO NOT WANT TO SPEND TIME WITH YOU, AND MOST OF THEIR OVERTIME IS SPENT DRAFTING BREAK-UP EMAILS THAT USE PHRASES LIKE 'IT'S BEEN FUN' AND 'I CAN'T GIVE YOU WHAT YOU NEED.'

(Dad sometimes forgets to sign out of his email account.)

## 8.

## DON'T FORGET TO SIGN OUT OF YOUR EMAIL ACCOUNT IF YOU HAVE SOMETHING TO HIDE.

I don't think Dad has ever been caught out over this in a relationship. But it is a lesson I learned from him that would stand to me if I were ever to conduct a torrid Internet affair, possibly with a sexy knight I had met online one day when my sexy Viking was off pillaging.

## 9.

## DO NOT SCHEME TO HAVE SOMEONE'S BABIES AS A LAST-DITCH ATTEMPT TO KEEP THEM.

This rarely works, although in the event of it failing you do get a baby, so it's not all bad. Unless you hate babies. In which case, you messed up.

## 10.

## DO NOT PRESSURE SOMEONE TO DO THINGS THEY ARE NOT READY FOR.

Dad is pressuring Hedda to commit. I suppose the comparable scenario would be if I pressured Felix to make sweet love to me right here, right now. I'm not ready for sweet love, though, and I have no idea if he is.

But, like, if I was and he wasn't, then pressuring him would be a really bad idea. Dad is in the process of learning this the hard way, but he is also teaching me a valuable lesson about how not to suck at being in a relationship. Thanks, Fintan!

Mum was not as grown-up as Dad evidently is. She understood the creepy cowboy/businessperson connotations of the word partner. Actually, Dad would probably only LOVE to be a cowboy/businessperson.
He's already half of one.

# 1.
# DON'T GET PREGNANT AT NINETEEN.

I know that if Mum had followed this advice, her life would have been very different and my life wouldn't have been, full stop. But maybe if she hadn't let my dad knock her up when she was still in college she would still be alive today. I hope I do not get pregnant while I am still a teenager. Twenty-five is the youngest I want to have a baby at. The absolute youngest. Although I would like to have done the deed well before I am twenty-five, because I intend to have a slew of lovers so I can shock people when I am old by being full of mad and filthy anecdotes about what I got up to back in the day.

I will get a sign made saying, 'Will reminisce for gin' and sit in the old folks' home crocheting doilies. (One of my many lovers will run a sort of crafting commune and that is where I will be taught to crochet by a naked Slovakian playwright named Fatwa.) I will also be editing my memoirs so that the boring bits are few and the exciting bits are many. Perhaps my grandchildren will visit me and I will pass on sage advice. 'Don't get pregnant at nineteen like your great-grandmother did,' I will croak wisely. And they will nod and be a little bit afraid of me and hope to God I don't start in again on the story about how I learned to crochet.

## 2.
## DON'T GO OUT WITH SOMEONE WHO IS OLD ENOUGH TO BE YOUR FATHER.

Sixteen years is the maximum age difference allowable when you are both adults, but it is lower than that for teenagers. They have to be in secondary school if you are also in secondary school, or a maximum of three years older. Otherwise there is something a little bit off. A little bit 'stranger danger'.

I don't know if Mum regretted her relationship with my father. She was angry at him for a long time and if it hadn't been for me they would probably not have stayed in touch after what passed between them had fizzled roughly out. It is weird, though, that I have a tendency to fancy older boys, like Felix and He Who Must Not Be Named (the other one, not Voldemort). Maybe I get that from Mum.

## 3.
## IF SOMEONE TEXTS YOU TWENTY TIMES IN ONE DAY, EVEN THOUGH HE IS A GROWN-UP MAN, HIS NAME IS PROBABLY ANDREW AND YOU SHOULD NOT AGREE TO LET HIM TAKE YOU TO DINNER OUT OF PITY.

'No dinner is worth listening to Andrew,' Mum said to me when she came back, brandishing a bottle of wine and a packet of Custard Creams.

## 4.

## IF YOU LIKE SOMEONE ENOUGH YOU WON'T HAVE TO 'WORK ON BEING ME RIGHT NOW'.

## 5.

## BAD BOYFRIENDS MAKE FOR GOOD STORIES.

And Mum was great at spinning yarns. For example, were she alive to tell the story of Andrew today, he would probably have texted fifty times in one day even though he was a grown-up man. For comic effect.

Sorrel is another one who has had some crazy relationships. She once dated a blacksmith and found it really hard to break up with him because no matter how often he cancelled plans, he was still a blacksmith. A blacksmith!

## 6.

## DON'T STAY WITH SOMEONE JUST BECAUSE THEY HAVE A RIDICULOUSLY COOL JOB/CAR/BAND/GROUP OF FRIENDS.

Unless they are a blacksmith, in which case give it six weeks so you can boast about it.

## 7.
## IF YOU DON'T WANT TO STAY WITH SOMEONE, BUT STILL WANT TO BE FRIENDS, BE REALLY NICE TO THEM AND GIVE THEM LOADS OF SPACE FOR A WHILE.

This is how Mum dealt with Hairy Dave who gave me Roderick. She used to say that Roderick and I saved their friendship because when they ran into each other they always had something neutral to talk about.

## 8.
## IF YOU HAVE A DAUGHTER AND SHE DOES NOT LIKE THE MAN THAT YOU ARE SEEING, YOU SHOULD PROBABLY BREAK UP WITH HIM BECAUSE DAUGHTERS ARE WISE AND ALSO YOU CANNOT BREAK UP WITH THEM.

Mum really listened to me and trusted my opinion because it was just the two of us and if someone was around a lot, I was going to have to be in their company as well.

I think that's why Dad's lack of disclosure with the Hedda thing annoyed me so much at first. Mum always analysed everything with me. Or everything that was suitable for my childish ears to analyse anyway. I imagine she did edit.

## 9.

## MEN WHO PICK ON YOUR APPEARANCE AND COMPLIMENT YOUR FRIENDS IN A FLIRTY WAY MUST BE DESTROYED.

This is something I did not need Mum to teach me, but she still did. Méadhbh was going out with a horrible man before her husband, Iain. Mum and Sorrel used to worry that he was a domestic-violence case waiting to happen. He broke up with Méadhbh on her birthday and she stayed in our house for a week and a half, sobbing on the sofa.

## 10.

## IF A MAN BREEDS RATS, HE IS PROBABLY LOVELY, BUT YOUR RELATIONSHIP WILL NOT LAST.

In retrospect, I kind of wish it had. Dave was one of my favourites out of all Mum's boyfriends.

## THINGS COME TO THIS, LIKE RUSHES OF BLOOD (1, 4)

Dad is taking the day off work today. And I am not allowed to go to school. He is calling it a mental health day. Hedda broke up with him, very nicely, last night. She said she was happy spending time with him once or twice a week but she was not looking for anything serious and he was, so it was not fair to keep stringing him along.

Dad's mind is kind of blown. I think, deep down in his stupid little heart, he imagined ALL women EVERYWHERE were only DYING to get married, especially to a man as wealthy and powerful as himself.

'I don't understand it, Prim. What did I do wrong?'

He moans constantly, in between bites of the sausage sandwiches and cups of tea I make for him.

'Um ... you tried to get her pregnant without her consent.'

'Only for about a week, before you stopped me. And I don't think she even knows about that.'

'She probably does. Women can sense these things.'

'Oh, Christ.'

CHOMP, CHOMP, CHOMP.
CHOMP, CHOMP, CHOMP.

'Prim?'

'Yes, Dad?'

'Can women really sense these things?'

'No.'

'Then what did I do wrong?'

He does not understand, this father of mine, that wrongdoing does not hinge on being caught. If someone tries to get a tree secretly pregnant in the woods without anyone else around to see or hear it, it is still wrong. And more than a little stupid.

I did try to make him understand, I really did. But there's not much I can say that doesn't begin with the phrase 'Women can sense desperation, Fintan, and they don't like it.' That is not a productive thing to say to the Moustachioed One right now.

I tried to get him to delete her number from his phone. Mum used to do this sometimes. We would write the number on a piece of paper and seal it away in an envelope, which she would give to a third party, usually me or Méadhbh. (Sorrel would always give it back to her too quickly because she is a romantic and easily swayed.) Mum was not allowed access to the envelope until she could give a good reason for wanting it.

Dad did not like the envelope idea. He has not texted her today but he keeps looking at his phone intently. I have texted him five times today.

Not from Hedda.

Still not Hedda.

Hi, this is your daughter, Prim. You are a wonderful father and Hedda is too good for the likes of you. ☺

Hi, this is Hedda. I was so wrong to break up with you. Let's get back to-

> gether. Meet me at nine in our special place.

(This one was a bit mean, especially because he didn't realise it was from me right away.)

> I know you said you didn't want to be disturbed but do you want a cup of tea? Also, maybe you can take up the zither again. Silver lining!

He did want a cup of tea. Hedda has messed with his head immeasurably. He is usually a coffee drinker.

It is very strange taking care of my father after his heart has been broken into smithereens by a lady I was always pretty sure was too good for him.

We have listened to a LOT of a band called Joy Division today. Joy Division are not particularly joyful. But they make a good sausage-sandwich-eating-and-complaining-about-Hedda soundtrack.

'She never loved me like I loved her,' he said at one point today.

And that's the whole crux of the situation. I would like to live in a world where you could easily gauge how into you someone was at any given point and, if your levels didn't balance, go to some sort of shop in which you could get them adjusted to avoid heartbreak and/or stalking.

I'd tell him she wasn't worth it but, to be honest, she probably is. Poor Dad.

I am trying to go to sleep but am being constantly disturbed by the sad little strains of a terribly played zither. At least he listens, this father of mine. At least he listens.

# A HEAD

Mary rang me this evening. She didn't want to talk to me in the house in case Ella accused her of snooping. Ella would have been perfectly right to accuse her of snooping. Snooping is exactly what she was doing.

'What is the story with this Caleb fella?' she asked, pronouncing his name as though it was some sort of horrible insult.

'What has Ella told you?' I asked, trying to buy time.

Mary was putting me in kind of a tough position, because, while I am a firm believer in Ella's business being Ella's business, Mary is all nice and mammyish and worried and I didn't want to lie to her. But Ella is my friend and so that is exactly what I did.

'I'm pretty sure they're just friends, Mary.'

'They've been spending a lot of time together, love.'

She calls me 'love'. This is how much of a mammy she is. It is very hard to tell a lie to someone who brings you tea and buttered biscuits when you 'have a face like a wet Wednesday'.

'Well, she really likes his ferret'

'That's not all she likes. They've been signing their text messages with Xs and sometimes Os. What does an O at the end of a text message mean?'

'It's a hug. A friendly hug. The kind that friends give friends. She often puts them at the end of texts to me.'

(No, she doesn't.)

'A hug, eh? That's a relief. I was worried it was some kind of sexting thing.'

**SEXTING:** Texting about you-know-what. I would not like to be sexting anybody because I have no interest in taking pictures of my naked body or seeing pictures of anybody else's just yet. And also, what if they showed it to someone? Eek!

**PETERED OUT:** Faded away, wore out, waned, died in the way that fires die as opposed to the way that people die. Words can peter out too; for example, this one day, I was talking with Ciara about Siobhán's new hairdo, which was hideous, and Siobhán came over to us, big orange head and all, and the conversation kind of petered out. Because Siobhán is friends with the Devil, but she isn't actually the Devil and we didn't want to hurt her feelings.

'No. No. Nothing like that.' (Who told her about sexting?)

And on that awkward note the conversation petered out.

Ella and Caleb are totally a couple, though. They hold hands in the hallway sometimes and he occasionally kisses her on the cheek. He has met and been well liked by Mr Cat. He still carves his name into things but he would never carve his name into Ella, so it is all good, at least for the moment.

Why shouldn't Ella have a boyfriend? If she is mature enough to be in school and go out and have friends and do the dishes after dinner three times a week, then surely she is mature enough to do other normal teenage girl things like have a boyfriend, even if he used to be an idiot man-bride of Satan and occasionally spat on people in his spare time. His ferret seems to have rehabilitated him, though. That and not being with Karen any more. And Ella seems to really like him, so I'm kind of giving him the benefit of the please-never-spit-on-me-again doubt.

Also, I want to do normal teenage girl things like have a

boyfriend and I'm kind of hoping that it is catching and that soon we will all be happily skipping about the place two by two, like an ark full of animals in love. It could happen.

It totally could.

It probably won't.

I rang Ella almost as soon as I got off the phone with Mary to tell her. Then I had to explain to her that she couldn't get angry at Mary right away because then Mary would know that it came from me.

'I'm still angry, though,' she said.

'I know. You should be.'

'It is none of her business.'

'She's only doing it because she loves you and is worried about you.'

'Why would she be worried?'

'In case you are going down a bad road, one that leads to cigarette-smoking and baby-making and spitting on people for fun.'

'Oh, he'll never spit on anyone ever again. I'd break up with him. Unless it was on someone who was cruel to animals.'

'Or Karen.'

'Not "or Karen", Primrose. She is not the Devil.'

'Yes she is. She is bright red and has horns and a tail.'

'Hmmm.'

'What you doing?'

'I am texting Caleb to see if he wants to smoke cigarettes and have babies together.'

'Ella! You are not!'

'I am. Mum will be incredibly relieved when she reads his reply.'

'What did he reply?'

'"No. Ewww."'

'Oh. Good. You're lucky he didn't take you up on that.'

'Luck has nothing to do with it. Everyone knows that babies are disgusting.'

'They certainly are.'

And then she was gone. Ella is kind of amazing. She gets things done.

I rang Ciara after I rang Ella. She only came back to school yesterday and she was all pale and worried and checking her phone constantly for Grandma Lily updates. It looks like she will pull through, only she mightn't.

Mac was in the hospital too. Apparently his granny is also sick. I wish his granny wasn't sick. I wish it was his dad.

Ciara met him at the café/newsagenty bit of the hospital, where they both kept getting sent for things for grown-ups who had forgotten how to work their legs. I told her not to talk to me about him and she was all, 'Why not? It's not like it was his fault that his dad killed your mum,' and then I think she realised how cold that sounded because she did a bit of a pause and said, 'Sorry.'

I told her it was OK, even though it wasn't. It was tactless. But people say tactless stuff when they're sad and people like me say tactless stuff even when they're not, so I think I was right to let it go. Ciara is my friend.

I wonder, though, if she would be so concerned about things not being Mac's fault if he were less easy on the eye. She is a biteen shallow when it comes to boys. But then again, so is almost everyone.

Also, Ciara thinks I was totally right to lie to Ella's mum about the whole Caleb thing. Because that is what friends do. Ciara has caught her mum reading her text messages quite a few times now. It is nosy and very wrong.

'We are lucky our lives are so boring,' she said.

But I don't think my life is boring. It is just filled with so much sadness. You know in equations the way what's on one side has to balance out with what is on the other side? If my life were a happy/sad equation, it would so not balance. The sad side would always be bigger.

I have maths homework to do, but first I am going to ring Joel. I have custody of Dad's phone for the evening and I intend to exploit the hell out of it.

Dad is on the sofa watching cowboy films on some weird cowboy film channel he has only just discovered. He changed into his pyjamas and took up residence there as soon as he came home from work. I made beans on toast with melted cheese on top for dinner because it is comforting and delicious. I don't know how comforted by it he was, though. He's barely said a word to me all night.

**BITEEN:** Hiberno-English for a little bit (not to be confused with a little bite). For example: "Have you even been paying the least biteen of attention?" is a thing that people who should be more interesting often ask.

I don't like having a sad dad. There is something really pathetic about him, all grey-haired and moping and gazing at John Wayne as if he had the secret of getting Hedda's hand in marriage and was going to tell Fintan what it was, just as soon as he was done shooting up those pesky Native Americans. Injuns, he calls them. I don't like that. It sounds like a robot.

Speaking of robots, I wonder if Marcus would like to come LARPing with Joel and me on Saturday? They're staying with us for the weekend, the two of them, and I'm not sure he will be safe in Fintan's tragic, wedding-ringless hands.

## A SERIOUS RESTING PLACE (5)

I didn't go to school today. I pretended I was sick and stayed in bed. Fintan was not suspicious because I never do this. He has forgotten about the whole counselling thing because of Hedda breaking up with him, which is the silver lining to the cloud of how boring and mopey and hard to respect he is.

I didn't have much respect for him before, Diary. But what little respect for him I did have has diminished. And diminished considerably. I did think for a while this morning that I might have actually been sick or something. Only I wasn't, so I decided to 'make the most of the day' and go on a little adventure, which somehow led to taking the bus and then changing to another bus and then, suddenly, as if by accident, ending up outside Brian McAllister's house, which was unexpected. I knew where he lived because he is in the phone book. What a normal thing to be in – the phone book. You don't think of criminals being in there at all. I probably shouldn't have committed his address to memory like a big old freak. It's just ... I can't forget it, what he did to Mum. And everyone else seems to have forgotten and it's not right.

We didn't even bother to visit Mum's grave last week. And that's such a little thing to do, to remember someone properly, to honour who they were just once a week and I couldn't even manage it with all the stupid unimportant drama that creeps in and takes up residence and tries to push my memories of Mum out. And there's so much I don't remember, days from when I was too young to have memories or just stuff that didn't seem important at the time. And if I had known, I would have honoured her every day.

Because I was twelve when she died, and that means I had about 4700 days with her, give or take a few where she had to go off somewhere or something. That's not a lot of days, is it? That tiny number doesn't seem enough. You would think your parents have MILLIONS of days with you, because they are your parents and their whole existence revolves around you, at least until you're old enough to be left alone and things. Even after.

Sometimes I still feel like I'm not old enough to be left alone. I mean, the things that I've been doing ... It isn't normal. And I don't know what it is or what it means. Maybe I'm going mad.

I feel like crying all the time. Only I can't. I've stopped myself from crying around people and in school for so, so long because I didn't want to be the sad girl, and I think I might have dried up all my tears. And the secret things I do – they feel like a kind of crying. Or like crying should be: private and secret and kind of a relief. Because when you are crying, crying is all you think about; there's nothing else coming in. It is just you and what you are sad about. At least if you do it properly.

I went to Mum's grave first. That was seriously the only place I meant to go. But then I kind of took a notion. I have no idea why. Probably because I'm weird and can't get over this fascination I have with the fact that he killed my mum and he still gets to live a normal life.

Eighteen months in prison. That's 547 days, or even less. A drop in the ocean compared to what he stole from Mum. I know he didn't mean to, but he did. And the thoughtlessness of it makes it somehow worse sometimes.

It was so random. There was nothing predictable there, no pinpoint where you go, 'Oh, well, maybe if she hadn't done X, then Y wouldn't have happened.' Well not from Mum's end. At his end X is drinking a feed of pints and vodka and deciding he was able to drive home. It was all his fault but he didn't do it on purpose.

'I didn't mean to do it.' Isn't that what little children say? It shouldn't be OK. I mean, it isn't. It isn't OK at all. I wonder does he ever think about killing himself? Because sometimes I do, and I do not have someone else's death upon my conscience. If I was him, I would have thought about it, I think.

I don't mean I seriously consider it or anything. Just sometimes it's so hard to be alive and I get so little from it that I think maybe it isn't worth the effort and I wonder how it would be to be dead. Like the way I sometimes fantasise about going on a long holiday to Marrakesh or somewhere, away from all my troubles. Not that I'd actually do anything about it. Or anything like that. I'm not really sure how I would do it. Mainly I just think about if it had been me instead of Mum.

Because it would have been easier in the long run, I think, if it had been me. From my point of view, anyway. And probably from Fintan's. He would still be living in his flat and going out with Hedda twice a week and she would help him through the whole being sad thing.

And Sorrel, Méadhbh and Dave and Frank and everyone would help Mum through it too. And she'd be sad, but not forever broken, gone and lost. She'd miss me. But I wouldn't have to miss her. I wouldn't have to keep on being broken. Because when he ran her down he broke me too and I don't know when I will be OK again or even if I'll ever. And it's hard. It's just so desperately, desperately hard that I don't know if I can even stand it any more.

I looked at Brian McAllister's house for a long time. It is nicer than the place I lived with Mum but not as nice as the house I live in now with dear old Dad. It looks kind of like a picture you would draw of a house when you are small: four windows in the front, white paint and a slopey roof that looks like a triangle. There's a gate and flowers that aren't daisies but are shaped like daisies and grass the exact colour of a green crayon. There is even a brown dog with a waggy tail and a round black nose.

And four happy family members. Well, three of them and one bad man. I didn't get to see them, but they were there. The fancy kitchen catalogue on the porch for Mrs

McAllister, the little bike with glittery pink handlebars for Mac's little sister. I think that she is seven, maybe eight. I wonder did she miss her dad when he was in prison? I wonder if they even told her what he did. That sort of thing would be a lot for a little girl to deal with.

By the time I got home it was getting dark. Dad worked late, though. I was still in bed when he got back. He asked me if I felt a little better. I said 'A bit,' because I am going to get up and go to school tomorrow. But I don't feel any better. I'm worried that I'll keep on feeling worse and worse and worse. I'm worried that dreadful things will happen over and over again to the people I love.

So many random things can go so wrong. A stroke is just where this little tiny blood vessel in your brain bursts or gets blocked, then that's it. You have a stroke. Pop. A car hits you. Pop. You get rejected and stop putting your socks in the laundry basket, bacteria collect and you eventually die of a disease brought about by your depression-induced filth. Pop. One night, maybe soon or maybe years from now, Joel walks home with his boyfriend and they bump into a group of thugs and get their heads kicked in. Pop. Pop. Pop.

Everyone is a balloon, only filled with life instead of air, and normally, just normally every day, we are deflating slowly, puff by puff. But also there are pins in hidden places. And you don't know where they are but they are shiny and they are sharp and they are coming. I can feel them coming. People say it is a terrible thing when parents outlive their children. But I would have been more than happy to be outlived by Mum.

It isn't me I'm worried about, or it is but only sometimes. It's other people. Other people are the scariest things in the world. Especially if you love them.

I looked at the McAllisters' house long enough for it to mean something. I don't know why I went there. I don't think I was expecting it to change anything or make me feel better or more in touch with my feelings or somehow more balanced. So I don't know why I am surprised that it didn't do any of those things. All it did was give me an insight into the many challenges faced by the stalker. Like weather-appropriate clothing. And having to make a snappy yet unnoticed exit when a car possibly containing your stalking-victim pulls into the driveway. I don't think they saw me. And it is not like they are my victims. If anything, I am theirs.

Grandma Lily is doing much better today. Ciara texted me about it. She is happy because Lily is the only member of her family she can really talk to about worries or feelings or whatever. She feels kind of out of it and so does Grandma Lily, I suppose, having had to move away from her home and forgetting things that she was supposed to remember and being a bit of a burden to her children.

Not to Ciara, though. They kind of get each other. I'm glad that Grandma Lily is improving. I don't think there is room for any more death in my life. I've had it up to here with death and now it's time for life and vibrant things.

She's cut the rosary down to five decades now. Ciara says them with her by her bed in hospital. She says it makes the two of them feel better. A decade is like a gang of prayers. Maybe ten, I think. I am glad it works for them.

# GRAVE

After school today, Joel came over and he and I sorted out our LARPing outfits. Joel is going to be a fabulous vampire/wizard, in an all-black ensemble with a white streak in his dark brown hair and an old black cloak lined with red velvet that he borrowed from Kevin, who used to play a mournful vampire warlord before it got all mainstream. Joel makes a really good vampire. Mostly because of his sad puppy eyes, which are total windows to his lovely soul.

I am wearing a medieval-type dress that belonged to Sorrel. I texted her to see if I could borrow it, and she got really into the idea of LARPing because she thinks it will 'be an outlet for my creative energy'. She dropped it over and was having coffee with Dad when Joel and I got in from school. Well, Dad was having coffee. Sorrel was having Rooibos tea because she is on some sort of detox. Rooibos tea tastes rotten but Sorrel claims to like it. I don't think she does.

Dad was talking to her about Hedda, which is weird for him but not weird for her. Sorrel has this way of getting people to open up. Probably because no matter how idiotic they feel, she has been in worse situations. Also she's really kind and warm and all the rest of it, but I think it's her innate scattiness that made Dad talk about his feelings.

Anyway, the dress is perfect. It has a medieval criss-crossy bit that narrows down to a point at the waist and it is long, but it has two slits up the side for high-kicking. I am going to be a warrior mage. So I get a staff/wand and two throwing daggers. I'm putting red streaks in my hair to match my dress. Although I'm going to pretend that they represent the blood of mine enemies.

Joel is going to be a good vampire and my former lover. We used to be murderers together until he reformed. We plagued nineteenth-century Paris and Weimar Berlin, collecting occult artefacts and killing all who stood between us and what we wanted. And sometimes just killing people because we were strong and they were weak and the blood on our hands was more potent than the absinthe that flowed so freely through our hedonistic lives.

Also, I have a raven as my familiar. He perches on my shoulder and, if I tell him to, he will fly over and peck your eyes out. His name is Roderick and I invented him so Roderick could LARP too.

I am going to wear loads of eyeliner and be beautiful and compelling but also incredibly ass-kicking and independent. No man can win my heart lest I rip out his own and use it in the course of my terrible magicks. I am the kind of mage ninja who does that sort of thing a LOT.

I could maybe get into this whole LARPing thing. Which is worrying but also kind of exciting. I would like to have a hobby. I could get business cards saying 'Primrose Leary, half-orphan and hobbyist' typed up. I could hand them out to people who wanted to do pretend battle with me.

I am going to wear fishnet tights, black cycling shorts and lace-up boots and tie my hair in two messy bunches with scarlet ribbons. Kevin is going to lend me the weapons. Apparently he has a lot of weapons. Dad has a Samurai sword but I can't use that because you could actually hurt someone. The stuff you use LARPing needs to be not lethal. Because otherwise it literally would be all fun and games until someone loses an eye. Or an ear or whatever else.

Liam and Anne are away for the weekend again. Fintan offered to take Joel and Marcus so they could use this voucher they got for Christmas before it runs out. Marcus is fun; he can actually hold a sort-of conversation now and he really likes Roderick because he begins with 'rrrr' like robot and is 'spiky and climby'. This makes him sound like some sort of sentient cactus-ivy, but Marcus means it in a good way. And Roderick likes him too – he is nestled into the helmet bit of Marcus's robot costume, which got taken off because we couldn't hear what he was saying through the plastic. He was saying, 'I want to be a robot vampire mage.'

He is allowed to be one. We have made his costume. It is basically a robot with a cape, pointy teeth, a wizard hat and a wand. His is probably the best costume. We have even made up a story for him. He might be interested in turning evil, so he is on work experience with me, which means he gets to observe my battles and fetch me cold drinks.

Marcus was enjoying helping out while dressed in his robot outfit. He was mostly talking in beeps, mind. But they were happy beeps. The beeps of a contented boy child.

I wonder what my little brother or sister would have been like if Dad's nefarious plan had worked out as he wanted. I get on well with Marcus but I don't know if I'd like a proper baby-baby who cried at night and had to be changed and fed and everything like that. That would be annoying.

But also maybe nice? If there was an extra sibling, maybe Dad and I would feel more like a family.

Although I would have to keep my secret identity from Baby Hamilton lest he or she become embroiled in the terrifying world of the occult.

Joel and Marcus are sleeping in the spare room, and Roderick looks too cosy in his helmet to move just yet. I hope he doesn't wee. If he does, I'll probably rinse it out and not say anything. It'll surely be dry by morning.

Joel snuck in after Marcus went to bed and we had a chat about Kevin and how cute Joel thinks he is and how it sucks that he doesn't like boys, but how maybe he will in time because a lot of people don't admit they're gay, not even to themselves, for ages. So all is not lost. Joel can cultivate him as a friend and be there to swoop in sexily when the right time presents itself. He did not use the phrase 'swoop in sexily'. He said 'be there for him', but he did a thing with his eyebrows that was pretty filthy, so I knew what he meant. I don't know about Kevin. I think Joel would do better not to hope. Because hoping for something that might never happen can hurt dreadfully.

Just look at Fintan and Hedda. Or me and Mac. Or me and Felix. Not that there is a 'me and Felix', even if he was a good listener that one time when we pretended to nurse Mr Cat. Stolen moments. The time after Marion broke up with him and we had a chat. The time he was wondering what that song I was humming in the sitting room was so he texted me. There are about three other such instances. Our love is a love that will stand the test of time.

If my life was a movie, though, I would probably be a stone and a half lighter. Joel tried to argue with me about this, but it was cursory. I am a size twelve who has gone down to a ten out of misery, whereas actresses are normally size six. To be a size six I would need to lose a stone and a half (fact), possibly by amputating my liver. If I were in a movie I could be in a crazy love-you-till-the-end-of-time-but-alas-I-cannot-be-with-you relationship with Mac. This would suck because his dad killed my mum, and the thought of him and his family makes me feel physically ill. But it would have its advantages because of how easy on the eye he is.

And the bragging rights! It would be like making out with Edward Cullen or Santa or something. Nobody could top it. Anyway, I don't fancy Mac any more. But it would still make for a very good movie plot-line if I did. Joel and I spent ages imagining how it would go, and it didn't make me sad or weird thinking about it, because the me we were talking about wasn't really me, just a character with me-like traits that answered to my name and had adventures.

Fintan came up to make us go to bed and to judge our outfits. He was quite taken with the concept of a vampire-wizard-robot. I should not be surprised about how immaturely he is dealing with this break-up. He is not a proper grown-up at all, in spite of his high-stress, high-paying job. Maybe he has to be such a grown-up at work that he uses all his maturity up? Does that even happen? It feels like it maybe kind of could.

He made us go to bed. We didn't mind. It was one in the morning and we wanted to be fresh-faced and buoyant for all tomorrow's LARPings.

**MAGE:** This is just another, cooler word for magician, wizard. Mages are really clever and have insane banks of knowledge. Like me, they are probably really good at table quizzes.

**WEIMAR BERLIN:** A period between WW1 and WW2 when Berlin was particularly debauched. There were a lot of fishnets and eyeliner and people bursting into song about how much of a cabaret life was. Or so I've heard.

**EMBROILED:** This sounds like an important step in the preparation of a fish dish. 'First the fish should be properly embroiled and then ...' But do not be fooled! It does not have anything to do with cooking. It means to be involved in something, right in the middle of it. And it is normally not something good. You could be embroiled in the world of high-stakes gambling for example. But you couldn't be embroiled in punctual attendance of business studies grinds. Unless it was a front for some sort of high-stakes gambling. In which case, I tip my hat to you.

**BUOYANT:** All kind of floaty, like a buoy. This is a good feeling and may result in happy humming and impromptu little dances.

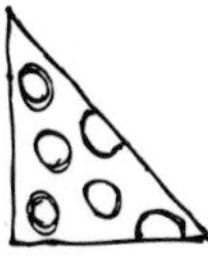

## THIS WORKS FOR WIZARDS (5)

We alighted in a forest glade at eleven o'clock, a vampire and a warrior mage. Joel can survive in daylight because I used my magey powers to free him from the tyranny of the blasted sun. We came up with quite a backstory. Quite. A. Backstory.

Kevin met us with a guitar case full of weapons, in full clerical garb. He was being Brother Shade, a Jesuit assassin. And looking rather ... nice. Is it weird that I fancied him a bit? It is, isn't it? It totally is. He was just so ... mean. And also moody. And also devout. We did battle a bit. I took him down. It was pretty hot.

There were about fifteen of us there, and Joel and I were the only new ones. The Game Master's name is Jane and she's a student. A Game Master is kind of like a ref in a football match in that they adjudicate if a dispute arises or if rules are broken, but also not like a ref in a football match at all because they actually get to decide what the rules are as well as enforce them. This system could readily be abused, but probably not by Jane, who is lovely.

I wonder if I were to bribe her could she sort it so I could do battle with Brother Shade more often? I don't fancy him when he is being Kevin. Well, maybe a bit, but it is only residual Jesuit Assassin hotness having rubbed off on him.

We used the dice and our foamy wimp-swords to determine who won. It was me. I won! I am awesome. Although I get the feeling that I haven't seen the last of

Brother Shade and Joel, melancholy vampire and reformed badass.

Other people I fought included

1.

A civil war soldier who was also immortal, Melmoth (real name Tomás)

2.

A courtesan and crusader for social justice who was also a fairy (real name Caroline)

3.

Marcus, the wizard-robot-vampire-child

Marcus won every battle he was in. None could defeat him. I think people were mainly being nice because he was so cute and well-behaved and genuinely thought that the activity we were engaged in was the coolest thing he had ever done in his life. Ever.

Even though it kind of wasn't, especially when people came by while walking their dogs as we were doing battle. Or when we got heckled by the homeless community. That sort of thing really takes the glory out of defeating a duo of warriors who have not been defeated since the dawn of time, and who are wearing a necklace of skulls. (Gloria and Mike: they are twins and they blame their LARPing on the way that their mother used to dress them both the same when they were small. This makes a weird kind of sense.)

Marcus wants to be a were-doggy next time.

'A werewolf?'

'No. A were-DOGGY.'

I bet Ciara would be AWESOME at making costumes for this kind of thing. Jane makes her own costumes, except for her corset, which she bought in a special shop in London that you have to be eighteen to buy stuff in. Oh, also excepting her boots. We are not shoemakers here. Unless you mean a shoemaker who is also a were-panther and who wields his cobbling hammer with the fury of a thousand red-headed stepchildren (Daniel, who may not have been taking the LARP as seriously as most of the others).

I might ask Ciara to make me some sort of villainous hat. I know she's not into nerdiness or drama classes – she HATES being put on the spot, because she's so shy – but I think maybe she would like the design aspect at least. And LARPing does not happen often, at least not reasonably sized LARPs like this. They tried to do it once a month but it has ended up being about once every six weeks and sometimes not many people come and it's harder to have fun with it.

I really liked hearing about everybody else's characters. And afterwards we went to the pub around the corner and Joel and Kevin and I had tea and everyone else had a pint or something drinky. Because a lot of them are, like, over sixteen and have fake ID. I always wonder how people end up getting fake ID. I asked Caroline and she said she has an older sister who looks just like her, so she was blessed that way. I don't think anyone would believe I was eighteen, though. I don't look almost grown-up. I look like a child with boobs.

Kevin is really nice, actually, if a little clean-cut when he is not in character. He's quite funny and he's going to lend me a comic featuring a character that he says looks as if my character and Joel's character had a baby. It's a girl and her name is Death. Which is kind of disturbing, but not as disturbing as the thought that me and Joel could have a baby together. Shudder. I thought about this because when I was ordering a stiff round of juice for Marcus, the bartender said, 'He's cute. Is he yours?'

To which I responded, 'No. EW. No offence, Marcus.'

'None taken, Primrose.' (He must have got that from Joel.)

We think the bartender was probably being funny. But imagine me as a mum. God, I'd suck at it. I can't even put a duvet cover on properly. Maybe she thought I was older, since I was hanging out with drinkers and stuff. I might have seemed like the responsible, tea-drinking mother, adrift in a land of pints and debauchery. Only, like I said, CHILD WITH BOOBS.

I don't want to look old for my age just yet. I already get pervy comments from men on the street sometimes. Things like 'Fine figure of a girl you are' and 'Give us a smile'. A smile is all I want to be asked to give for the foreseeable future.

It is hard being a teenager. See, we're not exactly children, so we can cope with some adult things and take care of ourselves, mostly. But at the same time, we still are children. I might be able to make lasagne, but that does not mean I am ready to pay taxes, raise a child or not get annoyed when the budget comes on TV and RUINS my cartoon-watching schedule.

I don't know. It was a bit scary. Joel and Kevin thought it was pretty funny, though. Me with a child. Boys don't get it as much, seeing as how they don't have to raise the baby until the mother is tragically killed by a drunken driver and the baby is old enough to do basic household chores and cook a very nice lasagne, now that she has figured out how to avoid the burning part of the whole endeavour.

I think Joel and me and Kevin are going to hang out again soon. I didn't tell Joel about how I might fancy Kevin but mostly only when he is being a Jesuit. I think it is better left unsaid. I mean, it's not like I am going to hook up with him or anything.

## STAFF

But also worrying...

I am a bad friend. Joel must never know about this. But how can I convince Kevin to keep what happened a secret without telling him that Joel fancies him too?

It happened on Monday evening. I was walking to the shop for a white chocolate choc-ice because it was sunny and I was finished my homework and Mary needed milk. Kevin was in the shop, buying a Tangle Twister. He lives right near Mary. His little brother was after making his First Communion so he had a bouncy castle in his back garden. I dropped the milk off and went over to bounce.

And bounce we did, two carefree young bouncers doing the most innocent, unsexy, completely unromantic, joyful, plasticky, brightly coloured, 'oh my God what is this feeling in my tummy' thing in the world. And it was sunny and we were both in our school uniforms and doesn't that sound innocent? Well, actually, there is nothing innocent about school uniforms. Their unflattering cut and questionable colour scheme provide an all-too-safe-looking front for all kinds of dreadful behaviour.

(Also, Satan wears one. Although she does accessorise it with a good deal more flair than the average student. People never seem to notice Karen's dress code infractions and I think it's because deep down they know that she could make them burst into hot, brimstoney flames with a single look from her cold, deadly eyes.)

Kevin looks a bit less together when he is in his school uniform. And he smells all clean and stuff. I don't actually think I fancy him that much. It was totally a one-time thing that will never be spoken of again. I'm a terrible person.

Anyway, we were bouncing and singing pop songs with the lyrics changed to be about people we knew. (We have several mutual acquaintances. OK, we have Joel. And the people I met on Saturday. And he did meet Ciara at the disco that time.)

It was pretty funny. And we talked about things – about Joel, actually, and how brave he is to be out so young and how hard it was for him last year and stuff. Kevin brought that up – I wasn't all telling of secrets or anything. Which doesn't make what I did OK. It just makes it not as reprehensible as if I had been planning it and also telling Joel's secrets to Kevin.

His parents were at home – his mum gave me a glass of apple juice – but the bouncy castle kind of felt like its own little world, separate from real life, where the rules and strictures that bind our society together no longer applied. We were in international waters, the People's Republic of Bounce.

And then he fell over and I rolled over beside him and he tickled me and I laughed and laughed and laughed and then he kissed me and it was everything a first kiss should be.

And also everything it shouldn't. Joel is going to kill me. I have to tell him, don't I? I have to tell him.

If only Ella had come over too. I did invite her. People don't get surprise-kissed in front of an audience. There's no way that this is all her fault, but I would really like it if it were. I need someone to blame who's not myself.

And poor Kevin has no idea that Joel likes him like that. So I am the only one who did something wrong. And it wasn't just a kiss. It was like eight kisses and one of them lasted for the guts of twenty minutes. I was almost late getting picked up by Dad. Luckily he was late too, like he almost always is.

Nobody suspected a thing.

I just got a text from Ella:

> You've been kissing boys. I could tell by the hair on you.

To which I replied:

I have only been kissing one boy. And what about my hair? Was it really obvious?

To which she replied:

No, I can only tell because I have been kissing a boy as well. The boy is Caleb. Who did you kiss?

To which I replied:

I will tell you tomorrow. But it has to be a secret. Because I am not supposed to be kissing that particular boy. It is forbidden.

To which she replied:

Myself and Caleb were forbidden for a while there. It was pretty fun. Is it Syzmon?

To which I replied:

No. How could you even think that?

To which she replied:

Because it would be forbidden.

To which I replied:

Makes sense. No, definitely not Syzmon.

To which she replied:

It's Kevin from down the road, isn't it? You wanted me to come bounce with you earlier. But I didn't and he totally kissed you.

And what could I say to that?

You are right. But we can't talk about it until after school tomorrow. OK?

OK. See you tomorrow.

I like Ella a lot. Ciara would have been like a dog with a bone. Maybe part of being autistic is that you don't gossip?

GOSSIP

Ciara met me at my locker this morning.

'What's all this about you kissing forbidden Kevins?'

'ELLAAAAA!!!!!!!'

'She texted me last night about your hi-jinks. What does bouncing mean?'

'He had a bouncy castle. That sort of bouncing.'

'Oh. I thought it might be a euphemism'

'For what?'

'You know.' She glanced around shiftily. 'Hanky *agus* Panky.'

I stared her down.

'That's Grandma Lily's code for sex.'

'Who told Grandma Lily about sex?'

'Probably Granddad Jim. Don't change the subject.'

'I have to. I can't talk about it at school. Most of all, you can't tell Joel.'

'Oops.'

'WHAT?'

'I didn't TELL-tell him. I just kind of intimated that you might have been kissing boys. BUT I said I didn't know the full story or anything.'

'What did he say?'

'He said we'd have to drag it out of you at lunchtime.'

And so he did. And he had to pretend like it was fun and OK and wonderful even though his little heart was breaking. I could see it on his face as Ciara oohed and aahed. I pretended the whole forbidden thing was because he was a LARPer and Ciara was annoyed at me for being so judgemental. She wants to come LARPing next time we go and she is going to help us assemble costumes that are even more kick-ass than they were the last time.

I said, 'It just happened. I had no idea it was going to happen,' helplessly around seven hundred times. Ciara nodded and said, 'That is the way of it with kisses.' Ella agreed. Her first kiss with Caleb took place across a very grumpy, very sleepy little ferret.

'We all have boyfriends now!' exclaimed Ciara. 'Isn't it great?'

Joel looked even gloomier. I felt sick and explained that Kevin is not my boyfriend, will never be my boyfriend, but she was having none of it. When you are as adorable as Ciara and someone kisses you, they automatically want to be your boyfriend. When you are as prickly as me and someone kisses you, it leads to dark and dreadful things that make you feel terrible inside.

Not that the kiss made me feel terrible. It was lovely. But that loveliness was supposed to be experienced by Joel, not stupid, grumpy me who hates herself and pretty much everyone else who isn't in her close social circle. And what I did to Joel, you wouldn't even do it to someone you hated.

I tried to get Joel on his own to talk.

'Let's ditch school and go to the graveyard and chat,' I said.

'I can't. I don't even want to look at you right now.'

'I'm so sor–'

'Save it. How would you feel if I'd hooked up with Felix?'

'Rotten. I know how bad you feel. I know I suck.'

'Then why did you do it?'

'I love you, Joely. I'll never ever speak to him again.'

'Fine.'

And with that he stomped off.

But later, he texted me. (This was after I sent him about seventy-eight texts reiterating how much of a terrible person I was and how sorry I am and how he's my best friend in the world and I know exactly how much this hurt him and what can I do to make it up to him and so on and so forth.) But later he texted:

You have to keep kissing him.

What???!!!

Because otherwise he'll KNOW.

He won't.

Prim, he is one of two people I've told I'm gay. If he kisses you and even though you like him you break off all contact, he'll totally know it's because I like him.

No he won't. I'll pretend I hate him.

If you want to stay friends with me, you'll kiss that boy.

OK. But Joel?

Yes?

He hasn't texted. Maybe he doesn't like me after all.

Aha!

Aha what?

I was testing you. Testing you to see if you actually like him and you totally do. We like the same boy. How weird is that?

Very weird.

I'm still mad at you.

I know. I'm just glad we're talking.

Sort of.

Any way at all. I'd never want you out of my life.

Prim? I kind of do want you to keep kissing Kevin. Is that weird?

I don't know. Maybe?

I get a sick feeling in my stomach when I think about it, but I'd rather he was with you than with someone else.

Ugh. Like Karen.

There's another reason I can't exactly be mad at you right now.

(This scared the bejaysus out of me, I thought he had cancer or something. I always assume people have cancer or some other death-inducing thing when they tell me that they have something to tell me. It is kind of a problem.)

I'm going to tell my parents about me this weekend.

OMG. You're so brave and awesome. Very proud of you and I'm sure they will be really supportive because they are lucky to have you.

Yeah, yeah. I know you're sorry.

Shut up! I would have said and meant all those things even if I hadn't made out with your boy crush.

I thought you only kissed him.

I did kiss him.

And?

And there was a very very small amount of under the jumper, over the blouse action as well.

Ewwww.

I know. He is clearly a damaged and tasteless sex-pervert. You want no part of him.

I do, though, that's the sad bit. Except when he's being Brother Shade. Brother Shade kind of creeps me out.

Brother Shade is awesome. That is what made me notice he was cute.

A Jesuit, no less. Now who is the sex-pervert? You are clearly made for each other. Filthy role-playing freaks.

Thanks for being so awesome about this Joel. I really need you in my life.

Shut up your stupid face.

No. YOU SHUT UP YOUR STUPID FACE, STUPID FACE.

Good night, Stupid. XX

Good night, Joel McStupidpants.

And that is apparently how friendships get saved. I still feel very guilty, though. Kevin hasn't texted. He doesn't have my number or anything but he hasn't asked Joel to give it to him either. I stayed in Felix's room and told

Mary I wasn't at home to callers after school today. She was quite annoyed/amused by this, because

1

She is not my butler

AND

2

I didn't have any callers.
I never get callers.

I am a big sad loser. I hung out with Ella and Mr Cat, doing science and watching him get wasted off the delicious catnip Ella grows for him. He was all purry and affectionate. He is a slutty drunk; all he wants are rubs and affection. Ella likes to let him have at the catnip every now and then because he is usually such a tightly wound coil of suspicion and greed. He barely lets anyone rub him unless they grab him by force and manage to reach the little spot under his whiskers before he leaps away, affronted.

I really like Ella and Mr Cat, but I also wanted something to happen. Because there'd been this whole big forbidden kissing build-up and it felt like tomorrow needed a new chapter to the story. You know, to take Ciara's mind off Grandma Lily. And also because it was weirdly fun being the centre of attention.

Maybe I should take up prize-fighting or MDMA in order to keep things interesting for my beloved friends and keep the focus all about me for my beloved ego. My beloved ego really likes when things are all about me. It is a bit pathetic. I am like Mr Cat on catnip, rubbing my head against legs and chairs and tables, purring/growling furiously for someone,

ANYONE

TO 'Love me, love me, LOVE me'.

Love

**MDMA:** A drug that teenagers in British dramas take. It is pretty much the same as ecstasy, I think, and induces plot-twists and feelings of euphoria.

# RING, SEAL, STAMP (8)

Hedda rang me today to ask if I wanted to go for coffee so she could break up with me as well. I said no.

She didn't actually say the bit about wanting to break up with me, but that was pretty much the gist of it, I think. Because I am bereaved and she was going to move in with my dad, she feels like she owes me something. She totally doesn't. I couldn't care less. Everyone is ringing me, actually. Sorrel rang to ask me how I was as well. I have many grown-up women who feel somehow responsible for helping me through Fintan's heartbreak.

Hedda was totally pumping me for information as well, though. She told me that just because she and Fintan have broken up, it didn't mean that she wasn't still 'there for me'. (Was she ever?) I wasn't sure what I was supposed to say to that. (Um, thanks?) Also, she said that she hoped I didn't think that she broke up with Fintan because of me. Then she went on about liking her life and her own company and not being a fan of the burdens and responsibilities that come with a marriage, with the result that I now totally think the break-up was at least partly my fault. She was digging herself quite a hole. It felt like she was breaking up with me over the phone because I had turned down her tempting offer of coffee. I don't even drink coffee. Anyway, basically she was, like, 'I'm sorry I didn't want to be your stepmother, but can we still be friends?'

We're not really friends, although she occasionally took me shopping for womanly things like sanitary towels and underwear. I don't think she will be doing that any more. Which is fine by me, because I'd rather Dad gave me the money and let me off to do it myself than someone hang out with me because they think it's like their duty or somehow charitable or whatever.

Anyway, she told me to ring her if I ever needed someone to talk to and that the door to her house was always open. What does that even mean? I know what it means, but it's a really stupid saying, isn't it? Unless you live in the countryside like Uncle Patsy, then the door of your house can't even be left unlocked when you're not home, much less open. You'd be robbed blind. Also, Hedda works funny hours, so chances are if I stumbled weeping to her door, barefoot and pregnant and needing to talk, she'd be off somewhere glamorous getting stuff done.

It was probably nice of her to call, but it left me with a distinctly guilty feeling, like maybe if Fintan hadn't got a teenage daughter with no mother to guide her, he'd have been a lot less eager to tie the knot/move in/have another baby with a woman who valued her independence every bit as much as he does (normally).

After we said our awkward goodbyes I went downstairs and made a pot of tea with real tea leaves. I stirred the pot and put about eight Bourbon Creams (my dad's biscuit of choice – bit boring, if you ask me) on a plate. I fanned them out artfully and arranged a cup and a little jug of milk on a tray. I brought it in to him in his study. He was not studying. He was snoozing. So I left everything on his desk, gave him a kiss on his big grey head and shut the door very gently on my way out. Sometimes I love my dad. Mostly when he seems a little helpless. I like taking care of people. It makes me feel like I can help.

At night in bed, I trace my fingers over the scabs on my legs. They feel like the mountain ranges on that globe we used to have in the sitting-room of our old house. Mum got it in some market; it was bumpy like the surface of the earth. It had a big pink USSR on it and that was my favourite part of all because it isn't a real country any more. I don't know why I liked it so much. But I did. The scab on the underside of my knee feels exactly like a piece of the USSR used to. Which is funny. Mum wouldn't find it funny, though. She'd be worried about me if she could see me now. Her forehead would get all squiggly with concern. But then again, if she were here, she wouldn't have very much to be worried about. If she were here my problems would shrink. And the biggest keep-you-up-at-night one of all would have disappeared if she were here. If my mum were alive.

I wonder where our globe went. Maybe it's in some other little girl's house now. Or gathering dust in a flea market, waiting for a home. I think about that, lying on my back, waiting for sleep.

## HOMONYMS

Joel came over and spent most of the afternoon on my sofa, crying. I hadn't seen him cry since we were kids. It was kind of disconcerting. His face got all red and crumbly and he made a lot of snuffly exploding noises. He had told his parents. His mum was fine. She said, 'We knew all along, darling.'

Then his dad was, like, 'No. We didn't.'

And,

'Are you sure?'

And,

'Maybe it's just a phase.'

Which wasn't too bad, but then his mum went mad at his dad, all, 'Well he'd want to be bloody sure, and him after telling us, Liam. Do you think he'd have done that at fourteen years of age if he didn't know it in his heart?'

And his dad said, 'All I'm saying, Anne, is –'

And she said that she did not give a damn what all he was saying was. Unless it was 'We love and support you – not in spite of who you are, but because of it.'

Then she had several ideas for what he could do with himself and none of them were pleasant. One particularly graphic one involved the leg of their piano stool, and now Joel cannot look at the piano stool. He is planning on covering it with a tablecloth or something. Anyway, in this way, Joel coming out erupted into a big dirty row that was not about Joel at all but about how Liam never remembers to empty the dishwasher, which is symbolic of intolerance somehow. He let them at it and called over to mine.

'What if they get separated, Prim? Where will we live?'

'They won't get separated, Joel. They're mad about each other. Remember the neck-kissing?'

'Ugh. Don't remind me. Maybe they would be happier apart.'

'They wouldn't, though.'

'Do you think I should not have told them?'

'No. You had to tell them. You can't live a lie.'

'I could probably live a little one if it meant that they didn't fight about me.'

'It wasn't just about you. You're forgetting the villain of the piece.'

'Dad?'

'No! Liam's just taken aback. I mean the dishwasher. That trumped-up little hussy's been nothing but trouble since the day she was rolled into your house in the first place.'

'You're right. I am going to give it a kick as soon as I get home.'

'Proper order.'

And so I spent the evening giving Joel hugs and telling him how wrong they were to make it all about them when they should have been supporting him. I mean, it isn't easy telling your parents something like that. I never discuss people I fancy with Dad. That sort of thing should stay well away from your parents, in my opinion.

Fintan came home around six and he was in rare form, not at all fazed by the daughter, rat and boy who had obviously been crying on the sofa in one big tissue huddle.

'What's happening?' (He still says things like this all the time. Once I asked him how he was and he said that he was 'chilling like a villain'. I think he thinks it makes him seem younger than he is.)

'Not much. Joel's gay now.'

'Marvellous! Let's all go for crêpes!'

So we did. Dad had a voucher that he'd got through work, so we ate for mostly free. It was this French-ish place, and they had cider as well. We were allowed some with our dinner, because Dad said it was so weak it was basically apple juice and also that it was a big day. He was very interested in Joel's being gay and asked him things like, 'How did this all come about now?' and, 'Is there a young man in your life at the moment?'

I was cringing at every word that came out of his mouth, but Joel was really nice about it and seemed to cheer up. I also cheered up. Mostly because my crêpe had three kinds of cheese and also ham and mushrooms and spinach in it. But partly because of Dad doing some really good parenting. It's a pity he couldn't parent me on that level. Also, Joel kind of told him about the Kevin thing! I was mortified and tried to kick him under the table but couldn't reach his stupid legs so had to content myself with pretending to drop something and giving him a big pinch when I went down to pick it up. He didn't flinch.

This is what he told Dad. Word for word.

'There is someone, but I've got a bit of competition from this one here.' (Jerks thumb at me.)

Dad nodded wisely and asked, 'So, this young fellow. Is he bisexual at all?'

'I don't think so. What do you think, Prim?'

'I wouldn't know.'

'Oh, I think you would.'

'Oh, I think you should ... shut your face'

'Primrose, don't talk to Joel like that on his special day.'

'It's not that special.'

'Yes, it is. Look at all the fuss we made over you for your confirmation and that doesn't really impact on your day to day life very much at all. You little heathen.'

Then I let out a big long sigh.

'Fair enough.'

We had crème brulée for dessert. I love crème brulée. It is the best thing ever. And it just means burnt cream but it is actually so, so much more.

Dad is totally going to ask me questions about Kevin. He does not know that Kevin is called Kevin. Joel was not that dim, thank God. Dad said that maybe he was better off not having anyone special at the moment, because it only leads to heartache and unnecessary drama.

I congratulated him on turning Joel's 'special day' into an excuse to moan about Hedda. Joel told me not to be so mean and asked Dad how he was holding up.

He said, 'You know. Good days and bad days,' and Joel nodded wisely, as if he had ANY idea what it was like to have your partner of almost two years break up with you instead of moving in with you. Ugh. The two of them!

I didn't really mind, though. I mean, it is nice that Dad and Joel get on. He offered Joel the spare room but we ended up dropping him home. His mum and dad had been ringing and stuff, so he didn't want them to worry or to get annoyed at him and start blaming each other and quarrelling. Sigh.

On the way home Dad asked me about seven hundred and eighty-six questions about 'my young man'. This is a really creepy turn of phrase because Kevin isn't a man, he's a boy. And also he doesn't belong to me, nor do I want him to. I haven't seen him since the bouncy castle incident. I do not think it was gentlemanly of him to kiss me and then not (at least) get my number and text. I mean, not that I wanted it to be a thing or anything. Because of Joel and also inevitable rejection and heartbreak. But I would like to have someone to kiss, at least for a little while. Someone to think I'm pretty and take me to the cinema or buy me hot chocolate in town.

# JESUS ROSE FOR THIS LONG-EARED PHILANTHROPIST (6, 5)

Almost the Easter holidays today. Three more days until two weeks off. Joel's birthday will fall smack bang in the middle.

After school, I went to the hospital to visit Grandma Lily. Mary dropped me and picked me up after two hours. It's on the way to Felix's guitar classes so it was handy. I hate asking her to do stuff. She's so busy already.

Grandma Lily was very thin and very pale and she was eating some sort of runny yoghurt-like thing that looked absolutely disgusting. I told her about school and Ciara making more hats and missing her dreadfully, and she couldn't really answer. I don't know if she even understood.

She, like, nodded and made sounds in bits, but there wasn't any kind of language I could decipher, and I really wanted to know what she was saying and I bet it was even more frustrating for her than it was for me and I almost burst into tears because I felt so useless, so I brushed her hair and told her she looked pretty. (She does look pretty; her mouth and chin are kind of like Ciara's.)

Then I didn't know what else to do, so I asked her if she'd like to say the rosary. She shook her head and pointed to the trashy magazines beside her bed, and so I read to her from them until Mary rang to say she was outside. I didn't feel too bad about leaving because she pretty much fell asleep right away as soon as I started reading. Ciara says Grandma Lily can't really follow stories and things that well any more because her brain is still all muddled, but she likes to hear voices around her because she gets lonely.

I'm glad I went. I wanted to visit her because she was nice to me and she is important to Ciara and a horrible thing happened inside her body and made it betray her and not be able to do the stuff it used to be able to do for her, no bother. It's probably a bit weird that I visited. I'm glad she remembered me, because otherwise it would have been *really* weird and I could have been asked to leave or something.

I spent most of the evening sending Joel messages of support. Things are still a bit prickly at his house. His parents got mad at him for leaving during an 'important family discussion' and he got mad right back at them and there was a lot of yelling and it woke Marcus up and he came downstairs crying and nobody got any sleep at all, between being grumpy and worrying about how grumpy everyone else was. He was so tired at school today.

He hasn't actually officially told Ciara or Ella that he is gay, but I'm not supposed to either. It's not that he wants to keep it from them, it's just that if he tells them at school, it'll be gossip-fodder. After what he went through at his last school, he has no desire to be bullied at our school.

Ella told me she saw Kevin at the shop earlier. He was hanging around, reading some sort of gaming magazine and looking a bit lurky. She nodded at him and he nodded back and this should not be as FASCINATING to me as it totally is. I wonder if he was lurking in the hopes of seeing me? Or maybe it is his sleazebag *modus operandi*. Maybe he lies in wait at the local shop and

**MODUS OPERANDI**: The way you work. It is Latin and Dad says it sometimes because when he was at school they all had to do Latin even though no one really speaks it. Except for phrases like *modus operandi* and *carpe diem*, which means 'seize the day' and is on T-shirts sometimes.

seduces young girls with the promise of bouncing and tickles? I hope that isn't it. I would feel all used and dirty and so on and so forth.

Not that I have anything used and dirty to be ashamed of. I mean, I'm probably one of the only girls in my year who hasn't been kissed more than once.

Except by Joel. Actually, I'm going to text him now.

## EASTER BUNNY

Remember when you kissed me like a ridiculous pervert because you wanted to impress the idiots in your year? ☺

Remember when you kissed the boy you knew I fancied on a bouncy castle like a heartless lady prostitute? ☺

I think that last ☺ was a bit passive aggressive. And I don't like it. ☺

Passive aggressive? Me? ☺ ☹

Do you want to call over on Thursday evening with Ciara, strange boy. ☺ (subtext free)

I'd love to

(No ☺?! Perhaps he is frowning.)

Oh, sorry. ☺

Phew. Was worried there for a second. ☺ Perhaps you can tell Ciara about your sexuality. ☺ Then smile as she gives out to me over the Kevin thing.

By sexuality, do you mean HOMO sexuality? ☺

Yes, Joel. You can tell Ciara about your HOMOsexuality. As opposed to my HETEROsexuality. ☺

Thursday is gayday. ☺

As opposed to payday. 😜

Or mayday. 😜

I think henceforth, we shall refer to Thursday as HOMOsexual revelation day ☺

Who are you calling a HOMOsexual? ☺

You. You big gay. ☺

I love you, Prim. ☺

I love you too, Joel ☺, but not in a HETEROsexual manner. In a you-are-my-best-friend manner. I would not tolerate being called a heartless lady prostitute by anyone other than you. ☺☺

Double smiley face? Bit needy. ☺

That's because I NEED you ☺☺☺☺☺☺ ☺☺☺☺☺☺☺☺☺☺☺☺☺☺☺☺☺

Oh. Right. Good luck with that. ☺

I didn't reply to that because I could not top my twenty-three consecutive smiley faces. Unless it was with twenty-four consecutive smiley faces. And my thumbs would probably be wrecked by the end of that.

## YOU ARE BORN ON ONE (8)

I am off school. And I got to see Kevin again. We did not kiss, but I think that we might well do so in future.

I went to the shop to buy bread. Mary was asking Felix but I leapt up and exclaimed, 'I'll do it!' in a helpful yet demented manner.

Anyway, Kevin was not at the shop, but he was walking his uncle's dog on the way to the shop. His uncle is in Spain for the month for something work-related so Kevin and his family are minding his greyhound, Theo, which is short for Thelonious Monk. I have no idea who that is, but isn't it the coolest name you have ever heard of, ever? I might have to change my own name to Thelonious Monk as soon as it is legal. I think it's eighteen you can change your name at.

I don't know anyone who has changed their name. Although I have my suspicions about Mum's friend Sorrel, whose parents are farmers from Carlow. Sorrel is not the name of a farmer's daughter from Carlow, but rather the name of a sort of eco-fairy. It suits her so precisely that I think it might be a self-appointed name. She probably grew up as a Padraigín or a Margaret. I must give her a buzz to thank her for the dress and ask if she has any other LARP-appropriate hand-me-downs to pass on to her late friend's daughter.

Mum was quite often late, actually. Isn't it weird that when you say 'the late' whoever, it has nothing to do with time-keeping and everything to do with their being dead? Although I suppose dead people don't really go to anything so it's not like they're ever early. Except for their death, maybe. Mum died too early, I think. But I don't like to think about that much because it makes me the kind of angry where I fill up with hate like a sippy-cup full of vitriol.

Thelonious and Wayne Rooney, Kevin's family's real dog, do not get along and must be walked separately. Thelonious has no problem with Wayne, mind you. But for some reason Wayne hates Thelonious. Kevin thinks it is because Thelonious's presence in their home forces Wayne to acknowledge that he is, in fact, a small dog. Wayne normally acts like a much bigger dog, all swagger and bark and being the boss of everything, and it must be tough, mustn't it? To have to accept that you aren't as big and strong as you would like to believe. Particularly when that realisation is highlighted by a dog three and a bit times your size.

Thelonious is a very calm, lazy dog and doesn't really care that Wayne Rooney hates him. He just lazes and eats and goes for walks and sometimes chews his big rubber bone in an unobtrusive manner. Each of these things is another twist of the jealous knife that has lodged in the tiny chest of Wayne Rooney. He steals Thelonious's food and toys, commandeers his basket, snaps at him and in general makes a nuisance of himself. Thelonious could not give less of a toss, which galls the tiny Wayne all the more.

Kevin does not know why his uncle continues to leave Thelonious with them, knowing how damaging it is to Wayne's fragile Jack Russell ego. I am not really a fan of Jack Russells myself. They were bred as ratters initially and because of that they all seem to be massive toolboxes.

I did agree to walk Wayne with Kevin, though, because I was at a loose end and wanted to talk to him for a bit more. So I dropped off the bread while he replaced one dog with another.

Kevin was looking like a defrocked Brother Shade in jeans, runners, a Radiohead T-shirt and sunglasses with tortoiseshell frames. His hair had no product in it and it looked ridiculously soft. I wanted to run my fingers through it and have him smile at me. His top teeth are really even, but the bottom ones are all crooked and he has one growing in front of another one, the way sharks' teeth do. For some reason I like his bottom teeth more than his top ones. Maybe because they would help me pick him out of a line-up. Or identify him by his dental records if he were to get murdered.

HOT.

I made Ella come with me on the walk. She insisted on bringing Mr Cat along as well. He has a leash, and she has trained him to take walks on it. This took months, so she was keen to show off his mad skills.

Wayne Rooney initially tried to act the fool around Mr Cat, all 'Bark! Bark! Bark!' but Mr Cat just looked at him, like, 'Yes? I am a cat. What of it, lesser being?' (This is how Mr Cat looks at almost everyone.)

And eventually, after a single disciplinary paw-swipe, Wayne was ready to act like a grown-up dog instead of a horribly needy puppy. We went up past the primary school and all around the green and it was lovely, the five of us in the sunshine, chatting and panting and wagging and walking. At the green, we took Wayne Rooney off the leash and threw tennis balls for him until he was in a frenzy of joy. So much attention! Such things to chase! He hardly knew what to do with himself. He kept running between us being all, 'I'm a happy dog! I'm such a happy, stupid little dog!'

It was lovely and made me warm to him, even though he would probably attack my beloved Roderick if their paths ever crossed. I reckon Roderick could get away pretty easily, though. Because he can climb things and dogs can't really do that.

Mr Cat was off the leash as well, and Ella was scratching his back in a way that he particularly enjoys. His purrs were deeper than growls, and I think he also liked watching poor stupid Wayne Rooney retrieve the ball time and time again. You wouldn't catch Mr Cat doing that sort of thing.

Roderick will fetch occasionally, but only with food or toys he particularly loves. And he won't bring it back.

Just fetch it and use it for his own purposes. I love my rat. He is the best pet ever.

Anyway, just before I went back into Mary's, Kevin asked me for my number and said that maybe we could do something at some point. I said, 'That would be good' even though he did not specify what this something might be. I hope it's kissing! I think he might have been a bit nervous, actually; he got all mumbly and his voice went a bit deeper than it normally does. Ella approves of him. She told me so once we went in and had a cup of tea.

'I approve of him, Primrose,' she said.

And then I went on for a bit about how lovely he is. I wish I could tell her about the whole Joel thing.

Gayday did not happen on Thursday. Ciara had to go to the hospital and visit Grandma Lily, and Joel and me watched a film about robots and didn't talk about the fact that we are both crushing on the same boy. Normally, I would have rung him as soon as I got home and gone over every single detail of what Kevin said and what I said back and how I probably came across like an idiot but I didn't care because I had so much fun, but I can't do that. Because it would be smug of me, and totally inconsiderate.

I feel pretty inconsiderate already. I mean, if the situation were reversed, I'd like to think that I would be supportive, but my main reasoning for that is that there is only a teeny tiny portion of the world that is gay compared to the big huge dollops of straight people you get all over the place. So it would be selfish of me to deny Joel the right to a lovely gay man he could go to the cinema and have mutually pleasurable gay loving with, based on my unrequited attraction alone.

But the situation isn't reversed. It is the right way round and I feel like I shouldn't be acting the way I am and I know I could help it if I wanted to but Joel is pretending that he is cool with it and I'm growing to really like Kevin, and I know that this is really childish and stupid but I kind of really want a boyfriend, in the same way that I wanted an iPod Touch for ages and ages and ages. Everyone else has one and I feel a bit left out. And, believe me, I know how idiotic that sounds and how little of a reason that is to screw over the boy who has been my best friend since I was three years old.

I can't do anything with Kevin, can I? It wouldn't be right. At all. But all the same, I want to see him more and more and spend more time around him. Even if we can't be together in a boy–girl type of way, maybe we could be friends. I think he would be a good friend to have. He is broad-shouldered and kind to dogs and these are fine qualities to have in a friend.

I should just go back to crushing on Felix. Maybe, if I actually managed to do some kissing with him, my Kevin feelings would go away. I must come up with a

SEDUCTION PLAN! Ciara would be the ideal person to ask about SEDUCTION and PLANS but she doesn't know why Kevin and I can never, ever be. Hurry up, Joel, and tell her, before I accidentally make sweet love to your boy-crush right in the middle of the green as Wayne Rooney softly dry-humps a football under a star- and-streetlamp-lit sky.

## BIRTHDAY

Joel is fifteen now, and his parents are giving him the gift of not being awkward around him for one whole day. Things are looking up, actually. Liam gave him a big talk about how OK he was with Joel being gay. Joel didn't go into what was said, but he was pleased with it and feels less weird around his dad now.

For his birthday, a big gang of us went for pizza. Me, Ciara, Syzmon, Ella, Caleb, Kevin and Joel's cousin Glen. It was really nice and while we were getting ready to go out, Joel told Ciara and Ella about how gay he is. They were very supportive. Ella even gave him a hug, and she does not hug easily. This means I can tell them about the whole Kevin thing now, but I am not sure that I want to because I do not come off well in that story.

I am going to meet him some time this week. We chatted a bit last night, but I made a point of not sitting right by him, even when Ciara made eyebrows at the seat beside him in a pointed manner that she probably thought was subtle. She also started a lot of sentences with

'Sooooo, KEVIN ...' It made me wish for a quick death.

Kevin tried to hold my hand on the way from the restaurant to his mum's car, but I kind of pretended I didn't notice and asked him several stupid distracted questions about how Thelonious Monk could still be a greyhound even though he wasn't coloured grey but more of a golden brown, like a pale shade of cinder toffee. Joel noticed, though. We had a talk, and he is still saying it is OK for me to 'go for it' with Kevin, but in this voice that isn't really his. This really jovial voice that masks his feelings.

I want Joel and me to be honest with each other because he is my best friend in the world. But when he was getting bullied, he didn't tell me for ages, and now there's this and he isn't telling me how he really feels and that is basically a lie. Worst of all, I think I'll end up going along with it and starting to see Kevin. I don't know why it is, but having someone think I'm pretty is really soothing. Because deep down in my tummy (I think my soul lives in my tummy, because my deep love of biscuits goes beyond the physical), I know that I am ugly. Inside and out. There is this need in me to be the cleverest, the most superior, and I'm really, really not. I shouldn't even be allowed around people. People are delicate, wonderful things and my big gaping mouth is so crammed with negativity that it often comes spewing out and afterwards when I go home I feel like everybody knows that there is something wrong with me. I don't think anybody would miss me if I died. Not really.

There is Joel, but he'd get over it pretty fast because I am not being a good friend to him at the moment. Dad could just forget about me all of the time instead of some of the time, and Ciara would be fine and so would Ella. The only person who my loss would break is my mum and she is not around and when I get in head circles like this and cannot sleep, I usually wake Roderick up and whisper in his little ratty ear that everything will be OK even though he is small, and that he shouldn't worry. Because he shouldn't.

Roderick would miss me too, I think. I think he would. But rats don't live for ever. The average is two years and Roderick is three and a half and he might die really soon and I would miss him so, so, so, so much. Like, hugely. He lived with me and Mum and he makes me smile sometimes when I am sad. I am sad most of the time.

This is something I have not been honest with Joel about. The sadness. And the cutting. But how do you bring that up? I don't want him to think I'm some sort of mad attention-seeker. It's private. No one's business but my own. But it's not normal.

It is dangerous, actually. Because sometimes I do not want to stop. I want to tear myself to ribbons and to shreds and bits of bone. White and red and beautiful and terrible. But I can't. I can't.

Dad keeps bringing up therapists. Now that he is over his bump with Hedda he can focus on messing with my life again. I don't like it. I don't like group. I don't like Triona. I don't like talking about the way I feel because it won't change anything. No matter how many hundreds of euro an hour you spend, no one is going to un-murder my mother. I don't like talking about her. Because the way they talk about her, it is like they are picking holes, giving me reasons to be angry at her for being dead.

'What would you say to her if she were here?'

And all I have is this: *Don't die. Don't die. Don't die.*

I need to do something, though. I do. I need to do something before I break. Because once people break, you can't put them back together with glue and silver paint, like Marcus's robot costumes. My hands are weird in the moonlight. All veiny and bizarre, like the hands of an alien or a monster. Not like a girl at all. I can't sleep, here at Joel's house. I thought I could, because I was able to the last time. But I can't now. I sit up at night, thinking about things that could be better. Starting with my eyebrows, ending with the refugee camps you see on the news.

I know that there are people who have it worse than me. But I just can't seem to cheer myself up. Maybe it is time for me to return to old habits.

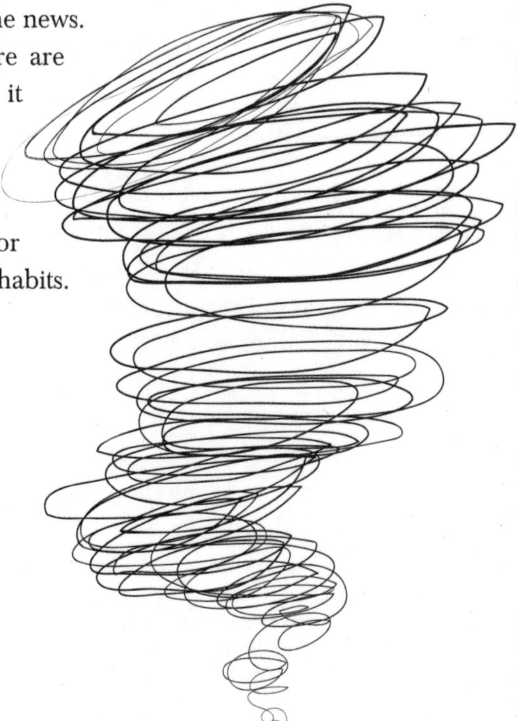

# THESE THINGS DIE HARD (WITHOUT BRUCE WILLIS) (3, 6)

I crept to Joel's room in the dead of night, brandishing spirit gum like a maniac. Soon, Joel and I were thinking as one. In sync, like ninjas we slunk through the house. Secretive and deadly. Once we were finished with our dreadful scheme, I cuddled in beside Joel in the bed. I know I'm not supposed to, now that we aren't kids and have hormones and urges and man-bits and woman-bits and all that. Actually, I think that policy might need to be re-examined now that Joel is a proper gay man who tells people that he is gay and stuff.

Anyway, there is something very comforting about his warm body. His breath, in and out in little spurts and snuffles. It lulled me, and eventually I slept. And in the morning, Anne and Liam and Marcus all had moustaches on. It was the best breakfast ever.

We are in a lot of trouble. Parents do not take kindly to night-sneaking and co-sleeping. It is not seemly. I think they might be worried that I will molest Joel. I was going to promise not to, but Joel stopped me before I got the sentence out.

In other news, all robots everywhere should sport moustaches. It adds a certain exuberance.

## OLD HABITS

Joel just forwarded me a text from Karen.

> Hear you are gay. Congrats! That is awesome. Want to grab a coffee some time?

How did she get his number?

'Grab a coffee'? We are in school together; it is not like they need to make plans. If she wants to see him, she can just appear near his locker in a plume of celebrity perfume smoke and brimstone.

So she likes him now that he is gay, and is trying to poach him. This is TERRIBLE.

Karen can be really funny and she always has stuff on. Joel might run away with her and not be my friend any more. I am his friend because he is awesome, not because he fancies boys. This is just one thing we have in common.

Ha! Just got another text from him:

> She = the Devil 😈 Be my friend, gay boy! We can clothes-shop and bitch about men like they do on the telly! What a tool!

Phew. It is nice that Joel saw through her right away. I hate Karen. She is shallow and hateful and full of spite. Joel does not need another friend who is shallow and hateful and full of spite. Not when he has back-stabbing, Kevin-fancying me.

How is Karen able to operate at all? I mean, that was SO shallow and obvious. If she had even a modicum of self-awareness she would be full of self-hatred and wouldn't come into school with a perfect face of make-up every day because she would be too busy crying big, oh-my-God-I-am-the-Devil? tears over various surfaces.

I hate her. I hate her so much. I need my Joel. He is on my 'people who would miss me if I died' list, which is a very short list indeed.

How could she be so thick? Joel is not like a sitcom gay man who says sassy things and tells it like it is. You don't come out and immediately start spewing out rainbows and fashion tips and soundbitey relationship advice. I want to poison Karen. All I need is poison and an alibi.

I texted Joel to ask for an alibi. He said he would swear that we were off shoe-shopping and being fabulous. I texted him back to say that I have never been fabulous in my life and he thinks shoes are boring, functional things of no great merit so no one would believe us except for maybe Karen. Because she is the Devil.

I hate Karen. And yet, I will not actually poison her. Curse my stupid conscience!

# A FOOD THAT CAN EAT AWAY AT YOU (5)

Grandma Lily passed away last night. I was at the swimming pool when I got the text, eating chips in the café post-swim. They have this amazing curry sauce that is completely bog-standard and made of E-numbers but combines with chips to form something greater than the sum of its parts. So I was eating chips while she was dead.

Ciara is very upset, I imagine. I rang and texted but I got no answer. But after someone dies, it's kind of blurry and fast and surreal for a week or so. I'm going to the funeral on Wednesday. And there's a thing in the funeral parlour tonight. You know, where people shake your hand and tell you how sorry they are. Which is stupid, because it is not their fault. And 'I am sorry for you' is kind of a patronising thing to say. Especially when you follow it up with not contacting me again, ever.

Some of Mum's friends were like that. Not Sorrel, Méadhbh (who has moved to Nebraska to curate something fancy, but Skypes me every month or so) or even Dave, who texts to see how Roderick is. (For Roderick, read me. Dave is not good at feelings talk.) But a lot of people forgot about me once Mum was gone. People who were only too happy to come over and eat her hummus or borrow her cat-carrier. We never had a cat, but sometimes we would capture feral ones and have them neutered. Mum thought that was the kindest thing in the long run, although she might have changed her mind if she were a cat.

Anyway, I was sadly eating chips when who should plonk down beside me, looking Hollywood perfect and mildly confrontational? Only Dolphin Laura.

'Haven't heard from you in a while,' she said. 'Did you lose your phone?'

'No.'

'Oh. Then why didn't you reply to my texts? I missed you at swimming.'

'Yeah. I changed days.'

'Why?'

'I had a thing.'

(I said this because I read somewhere once that being overly specific is the downfall of many a liar. Besides, I couldn't think of anything that wasn't 'I joined the circus'. And I clearly hadn't joined the circus.)

'Oh. What sort of thing?'

(Damn her! She is clearly a master of lie-unravelling.)

'A family thing.'

(This is clever, because it is a bit true.)

And she kept prodding and being friendly and then she stole a chip and that was the last straw, so I just came out with it.

'Laura, the reason I've been distant is because I haven't wanted to be around you. It's to do with Mac.'

'Oh my God. Did you, like, get off with him?'

'No! His dad killed my mum'

'Oh. That's much worse.'

(She didn't mean it, though. She was pretty pleased I hadn't got off with him. I'm not sure why that even occurred to her to be honest. Bit of a stretch. Also a compliment.)

'He doesn't really talk about his dad. I mean, I kind of only knew why he was in prison and stuff from my mum.'

'Oh. OK.'

'That explains a lot, actually.'

'How?'

'Well, you getting all weird and distant, like you said, and also that he was always talking about you and trying to find out things.'

'Really?'

'Yeah, that stuff with his dad really messed him up; he was pretty cut up about it.'

(Pause.)

'Although clearly not as cut up as you. I mean, you lost your mum. That's huge.'

'Yeah, yeah, it is.'

And we had a big talk and stuff, and she told me about her and Mac and how his father being back hadn't made things better and how his little sister was getting teased at school because her daddy was in jail, and all this stuff that really made me think. I don't know if it was productive thinking. And maybe it was because Grandma Lily was dead, but we both had a small bit of a cry. Hers involved delicate tears floating down her cheeks like small, shiny globes of crystal. Mine involved snot and a lot of facial contortions. I feel like I might have made a new friend today, though. Which is something, even if I don't want to see her very often – or ever if it means seeing her handsome, troubled, evil-father-having boyfriend.

I do feel really sorry for his little sister Tracey. It is hard enough being a kid with a dad in prison without getting bullied over it. When I was a kid, I used to kind of wish that Dad could live with us all the time. Not as Mum's boyfriend, because that would have been weird and wrong. But as my dad. I was jealous of Joel for having two parents in the same house when I only got my dad some weekends. I never got bullied for living with Mum though, because I didn't grow up in the 1950s. But you do miss your parents when they aren't around, even if they aren't your favourite parent.

Mum was my favourite parent. She had to be: I saw her all the time and Dad only sometimes. So clearly Mum was going to be the one I talked to about what I'd done at school and things I liked and what I was afraid of and all that stuff that brings two people closer. I didn't get to really know Dad as a person until I moved in with him after she died.

I think I know him now, at least a little. He is my friend as well as being my dad. Except when he wears socks and sandals when picking me up from the swimming pool café where I am chatting with my sort-of new friend Dolphin Laura. Then he becomes my enemy. Not really, but it was pretty embarrassing. I think I played the reverse psychology card pretty well, though.

'I like that you have finally given up on trying to be cool, Fintan. Loving the socks and sandals. You are officially old.'

'Socks and sandals are practical and comfortable.'

'Yeah, and stylish.'

'Stop it, Primrose, I have an ingrown toenail and I'm feeling a little bit sensitive about it.'

'Grandma Lily died.'

'Oh, Prim, I'm sorry. You looked like you'd been crying.'

He was driving so he couldn't give me a hug, but he talked to me about Grandma Lily and how sad Ciara might be and promised he would take time off work to go to the funeral with me. Which is something.

Joel is coming too. And Ella. I rang them both. I didn't ring Syzmon, because I don't know him as well and he belongs to Ciara so she probably rang him herself.

## CHIPS

Kevin rang this afternoon and wanted to take me to the cinema. That's what he said. Take me to the cinema. Like a proper date. I said yes, because I wanted to see him. And then I wrote three text messages backing out and deleted them. Life is short, too short to not kiss boys because of drama. But on the other hand life is short, too short to screw over your best friends by kissing the boys they like. It is a tough one. But the general consensus is that life is short, and you can use that to justify various courses of action.

After the film, we went around the corner of the cinema and kissed and kissed and kissed and it shoved all the death and drama to the back of my mind and I was just a mouth and he was just another mouth and we were kind of exploring each other in this really lovely way and it was so fascinating. You wouldn't think that something so repetitive could be so fascinating. And his arms were around me and my head was bent right back. I have a terrible crick in my neck now, but it was worth it.

I wonder would it be kinder to Joel if Kevin and I were friends with benefits, as opposed to boyfriend and girlfriend? My seduce-Felix plan has kind of gone out the window, because:

1. It is highly impractical.
2. I wouldn't know how to go about it.
3. Mary and Ella would cop what I was up to pretty much right away, long before Felix did, and
4. The humiliation. It would be great.

Also, I kind of like fancying Felix from afar. He is the one I will never have. And I kind of value the crush I have on him more than the relationship or kissing I could have. My crush on Felix is comfortable and familiar, like an old hoodie. I can pull it on when I am by myself and think about the adventures we would have if I were just a little older and just a lot cooler.

One of my favourite daydreams involves being secretly really good at electric guitar and he finds me one day, playing in the garage. Neither of our houses has a garage, but this is why it is a daydream. And he is all, 'Wow, I must have you as a bandmate,' and I have no idea that he has a big crush on me but he does and then we get a record deal or something and he brings me a big bunch of daisies wrapped in sheet music and we make out all over the place and eventually move to Paris where we have little messy-haired babies who we dress in gender neutral clothing, like cream Aran jumpers and little red cords and tiny little boots. Also our babies are all really good at music, and Fintan comes over several times a year and teaches them the zither.

Another one involves me being secretly really good at growing organic vegetables and ends with us opening an eco-café that is extremely cool and also famous for its soups. Chefs come from miles around begging for the recipes, but I am too busy making out with Felix and running a successful and beloved eatery to share it with them. I like my daydreams. And I don't think that I would be able to daydream about Felix half as well if he were my real boyfriend.

I have to stop kissing Kevin. I really do. But also I have to do a lot more kissing of Kevin and possibly be kissing him right now. I really don't want to grow up like Dad and hurt the feelings of people I care about, like my mum. I don't want to be that person. Maybe if we only hook up when we're in character? But that would be really sleazy and weird and could lead to the sort of latex nurse costumes that you see in the window of Ann Summers on O' Connell Street and are highly impractical, because how could you attend to a patient in something that tight and low-cut?

Ciara thinks they are dreadful as well. Sometimes we worry as to what will be expected of us when we are older. Not that we will have to do what men expect or anything, but there's just so much world and so many people and they all want different things and some of those things are really weird and some of those things are perfectly fine but don't tally with the sort of stuff we want for ourselves, and between friends and parents and boyfriends it would be really easy to get lost in pleasing other people and end up a very sad and lonely girl indeed. And the worst kind of lonely of all, lonely for yourself because you have forgotten who that is because it has been so long since you thought about what you wanted.

That is one of the things that is wonderful about Hedda. She lives for herself and not to please people.

I think Dad might have asked her to marry him out of people-pleasing, in a way. Like, she was lovely and he loved her and also he wanted some sort of relief from parenting me all by himself, and maybe now that he has a kid living with him and has had to settle down anyway, marriage didn't seem like such a big and scary step?

Ciara is especially worried about the whole 'changing her life to be what other people want' thing, because her parents have already decided that she is going to be a teacher or a psychologist – a teacher because she is good at babysitting and liked primary school ('Not enough to go back there for ever, Primrose!') or a psychologist because she used to eat her own hair and she could help others like her ('Why would I want to do that? My psychologist was no help to me. It is enough to make me nibble my plaits off.').

Ciara wants to study art or fashion design, and especially wants to be a milliner, but that is not practical so she needs to find something else that she wants to do and then millin in her spare time. Is millin a verb? I don't know. It sounds like the verb of milliner but maybe it isn't. It isn't as if dentists go around denting things all day.

I now need to do the job that Grandma Lily was doing and encourage her as much as possible. Because I would like to see her ridiculous hats on a minor celebrity someday. Or even a major celebrity, only you hardly ever see them wearing hats. Not at the Oscars anyway. Maybe the Queen of England could wear one to the races. There is a really lovely one that has a big round base with a netted veil made of the tiniest cut-out felt horses in red and mustard and purple and pink and blue. The Queen could wear that one because she probably likes horses if she goes to the races. It would be in keeping.

# INVOLVES THE WORD FUN, BUT IS NOT FUN, REALLY (1)

Dad wants me to go to something called cognitive behavioural therapy. It is not about going over stuff that has happened but about looking at ways to change bad behaviour patterns. Bad behaviour sounds like I am some sort of juvenile delinquent, and I really want to say it in a pretend dominatrix voice combined with some sort of whipping sound effect, but I suppose being sad and angry almost all the time to the point of screaming and other stupid things isn't really good behaviour, is it?

The things we do to cope with life can be positive or negative, Dad says. He also told me Mum used to see a therapist too, once upon a time, because she had 'dark moments'. (Would they have anything to do with the fact that a much older man went and got her pregnant? is what I wanted to say, but didn't. I'm kind of too tired to have a row about it.)

'You'll know more when I give you her diaries, Prim.'

'Can't I have them now?'

'Not yet.'

He is waiting until my sixteenth birthday, because on that day I will be magically mature enough to handle all of Mum's deepest, darkest secrets.

I don't know what they are. All I have is this: she grew up in the country, moved to Dublin for college, where she studied English and philosophy and met my dad on a night out at the beginning of her second year. They were together for about six months but it was on and off and on and off and during one of the 'on' periods (presumably) she got pregnant with me, and they tried to make it work because of that, only they couldn't and he broke her heart but she did not break his and they found it difficult at first but they had to see each other because of me and so they ended up civil, but never really friends. There was always a little bit of something brewing there. Resentment, I suppose. Remaindered heartbreak or the memory of pain.

I loved my mum more than my dad because she was the one who tucked me in at night. I think that now I know him better I am on my way to loving them both the same. It is hard for him to compete with a memory, though.

We visited her grave and I told her about Grandma Lily and Joel and Kevin and how worried I am about Ciara and also how I sometimes worry about myself as well and how I think I might need to do something, something like what Dad suggests. And I wish that I could talk to her and find out what she thinks would work the best.

If I were sad and in her house, Sorrel would come over and Reiki me. 'Reiki the head' Mum used to call it – she didn't really give it that much credit but still found it relaxing. Also, Sorrel likes to feel useful in a crisis, because other people are so frequently useful to her during her many crises. I wish I could fill in the blanks of Mum and Dad, paint a picture that's all colours and no spaces.

Mum's grave is clean and I pulled out the weeds that will not flower. Mum liked wildflowers: primroses for me, cowslips for her, daisies for happiness, bluebells for beauty, dandelions for bravery because they look like the manes of little lions. I leave the flowers Mum would have liked and pluck out Japanese knot grass, herb Robert and nettles. Herb Robert has a little flower to it, but Mum didn't like it because of the saying 'Never trust a man with two first names' and also the way it doesn't have a smell.

'Did you love Mum?' I asked Dad, my hands wet with earth and sap.

'Of course I did, because she gave me you.'

That's not an answer, more of a placatory soundbite. I need more than that from him today.

'But what about before?'

'I liked her, Prim, and I was attracted to her. But she was young, and there was too much drama in it and ...'

'And?'

'I kind of lost interest. I couldn't help it, and I knew that I was hurting her, and I felt terrible about it. When I found out about you ...'

'What?'

'I tried. I did try. Your mother and I were very different people. And not the kind that complement each other. But I think that we were meant to be together, because the two of us together made you.'

I don't really like the idea of being made. Like a cake or a salad. But I understood what he meant. We stayed there talking for a while, the three of us: Mum, Dad and me.

It was one of those days where I felt, instead of 'Oh, she can't be gone,' that maybe she wasn't gone, not fully. Maybe, somewhere, a vestige of the love she had for me was listening and watching out for me. I rubbed the letters hewn into her gravestone,

BELOVED MUM OF PRIMROSE

and felt lonely and not lonely at the same time. Things have a way of working themselves out, Dad says. Today it didn't feel like a big fat lie from a hairy-lipped liar. Today it felt like maybe it was true.

# FUNERAL

Grandma Lily is in the ground now. I wore my black sheath dress with the three quarter length sleeves and a pair of tights that didn't have a hole in. Appearances are important to Ciara, and I wanted to show respect. Joel had black cords and a dark grey jumper. He doesn't fit into his confirmation suit any more. Can't believe that was two years ago. It feels like yesterday or a lifetime ago. One or the other; not two years.

The funeral was lovely. Ciara met myself and Joel and Ella, Caleb and Dad outside the church. She had dark circles around her eyes and had three boxes. She produced three fascinators from them, each of them with a lovely big fresh calla lily on the side. Mine was blue and had a scissors, a ball of wool and a tiny bottle of gin stuck onto it, Ella's had an armchair, an old-fashioned radio and a paintbrush. Not the full things, you understand, little cut-out versions, but so accurate you knew just what they were.

Ciara pinned them to our heads and ignored the looks that all the people bustling in were throwing. I helped her put hers on last of all, just as her mum called for her. It was rosary beads entwined around a broken heart, covered in tears. She made them out of little beads of glue, the tears.

'I was up all night making these, for her,' she said dully. Her mum grabbed her elbow and looked at us as if we were insane. She didn't get it. Lily would have got it. Lily would have been so very proud of Ciara, of what her granddaughter's clever hands were capable of doing.

'I feel a little silly,' whispered Ella.

So did I, but I held my head high as I walked down the aisle and sat in a pew with bits of someone's life balanced on top of my head, saying more about Lily than the priest who didn't even know her to begin with. He called her Lillian, which wasn't right at all. Everyone who knew her called her Lily. Rising and kneeling, the hour passed like tides.

And back to the graveyard we went and watched as the coffin was lowered into the ground. Ciara was in floods. She almost doubled over at one point. Her mum had a hand on her shoulder, squeezing it. Her dad's mouth was a straight line. He looked off into the horizon. Maybe he was trying not to cry. I went over to Ciara and held her hand. I was crying too, because of Lily, but also because of Mum. She was in that same ground, fifty feet back and about five minutes over.

I hadn't been to a funeral since Mum's. And it was hard, but not as hard as I thought it would be. I don't think that my eyes will ever be dry, though, when the shovels come and cover up the coffin with the earth. It feels like rubbing out a life, removing the evidence, making them untouchable and so far away, too far away to reach. There is a body, then that body becomes a body in a box and then that body in the box becomes a body in a box in a hole and then the body in a box in a hole becomes a body in a box under the ground. Under the ground is not an easy place to get to, unless you are a badger or a mole.

Everyone went back to Ciara's house for sandwiches, but Ciara and I stayed. She told her mum she'd get a lift with Dad. She got the eyebrows but she didn't care. Ciara's mum has the most expressive eyebrows of anyone I know. She blackens them with kohl.

They were not happy. Dad went to the car and Ella and Caleb snuck off to kiss behind some yew trees, which are poisonous and practically immortal. The teacher who told me about birds told me that. I have been a bit suspicious of the yew tree ever since.

Ciara, Joel and I were hand in hand in hand. It began to rain and Joel said he'd meet us in the car and wandered off. Our lilies drooping, we walked and talked about Lily, who she'd been and how she would be missed. And then we were there.

'I want you to meet someone,' I said, and Ciara looked at me.

'This is my mum, Bláthnaid. Mum, this is Ciara. She's one of my best friends.'

'Hello, Bláthnaid,' Ciara said and knelt down by the grave.

We said a prayer together, holding hands. She asked my mum to keep an eye on Lily, seeing as she's new to the area and all. She plucked the lily off her fascinator and put it in the middle of the grave. On the way back to the car, I did the same for Lily. The damp, dark sky made all the specks of green on tidied graves seem brighter, pushing up and fanning out. Soon they'd grow through Lily's black earth too.

My ballet pumps were soaking by the time we piled in to my dad's back seat, two wet girls together being sad but also kind of close, her head on my shoulder. We dropped her at her house and stayed there for a while, eating sandwiches and trying to comfort and be comforted.

The hat is on my desk now, drying slowly. It doesn't really work without the lily. But that is probably the point.

## SOMETHING MISSING, SOMETHING MISSED. (3)

M
u
m

OK, so a lot of people helped me make this book by being awesome. Particularly the **LITTLE ISLANDERS**, whose energy, enthusiasm and dedication to making sure children have engaging things to read is an inspiration:

**SIOBHÁN PARKINSON** (without whom Prim would never have been born) needs no introduction so I am giving her an acknowledgement instead - she is amazing and wildly talented as well as being incredibly generous with her support and advice.

The incredible **ELAINA O'NEILL**, managing editor and all round lovely person, who juggles so many tasks with such inspiring precision that she makes it look effortless. I know it isn't effortless, Elaina, and I really appreciate all you have done for Prim. Thank you.

My **PARENTS** got a mention at the start of the book, so I'm leaving them out.

**TADHG**, my little brother, who read and liked *Prim Improper* in spite of being a tired young doctor and not a teenage girl. Thanks for being supportive and clever and hilarious and for giving my guinea pigs lifts from time to time.

**DIARMUID O'BRIEN**, ex-batman and current gang member, who listens to everything I write before anyone else. I love you. Hey-ho.

**CIARA BANKS, SUZANNE KEAVENEY, CAMILLE DEANGELIS** and **SARAH MARIA GRIFFIN** for offering writerly advice and warm friendship. I am so glad of you all.

My godmother, **CARMEL KING**, who taught me that you don't have to be loud to be brave.

My godfather, **JOHN L. SULLIVAN**, who is as generous and kind a man as you could hope to meet.

My grandmother, **ALACOQUE SULLIVAN**, because visiting her house is like walking into a hug.

To the brave, strong and cool as ice **MIKE GRIFFIN**, who inspired a bit of this book and also taught me how to hold a knife properly.

And finally, someone I forgot to thank the first time: **FIDELMA SLATTERY**, who made *Prim Improper* look so pick-uppable and and has done the same for *Improper Order*. Like. A. Boss.

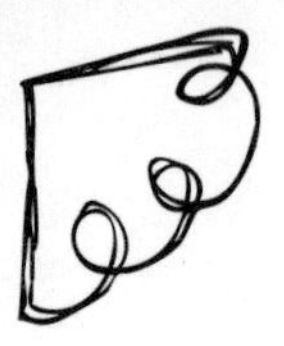

# PRAISE FOR DEIRDRE SULLIVAN AND *PRIM IMPROPER*

SHORTLISTED FOR THE BISTO CHILDREN'S BOOK OF THE YEAR AWARDS 2010-11

'...the best children's-fiction debut I've read in a long time ... Few authors can write hilarious books about serious subjects without awkward shifts in tone, but Sullivan pulls it off brilliantly ... an impressively assured and hilarious debut novel'
Anna Carey, *The Irish Times*

'[Prim] records with wit and style the highs and lows of her complex existence' Robert Dunbar, *The Irish Times* top 30 children's books of 2010

'Prim Improper distinguishes itself from its peers with its contagious sense of humour ... making a lasting impression'
*Inis* Magazine

'An exciting new talent'
Sarah Webb, author of the Amy Green series

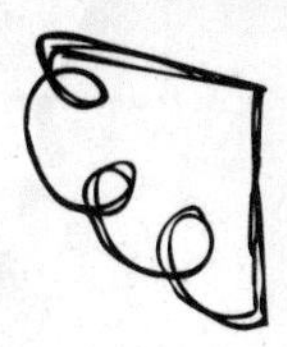

'A writer with a sparkling talent ... her first novel for young teens is even more hilarious and touching than I could possibly have imagined'
Siobhán Parkinson

'Hilariously written, very clever and an original, addictive read'
Mary Esther Judy, Fallen Star Stories blog

'Incredibly funny ... a star in the making'
Fiona Looney, author and TV presenter

'So original ... It had a sort of addictive quality to it - like you couldn't put it down!'
Bríd, 14

'Truly a great book'
Chloe, 13

'Really, really good'
Nuala, 11

'I love Prim's character and personality, she's so funny and spunky. Her precocity, sense of humour and attitude are really amusing. Thank you for writing such an excellent book that has made me laugh a lot and nearly cry a little'
Laura, 13